P9-BIV-123

ONE NIGHT

marsha qualey

dial books

new york

Published by Dial Books

A division of Penguin Putnam Inc.

345 Hudson Street

New York, New York 10014

Designed by Lily Malcom

Text set in Nofret

Printed in the U.S.A. on acid-free paper

1 3 5 7 9 10 8 6 4 2

Library of Congress Cataloging–in–Publication Data

Qualey, Marsha.

One night / Marsha Qualey.

p. cm.

Summary: Nineteen–year–old Kelly, ex-addict niece of a nationally–
renowned Minnesota talk show host, has an unexpected adventure
with the visiting prince of a war-torn Eastern European country.

ISBN 0-8037-2602-3

[1. Princes—Fiction. 2. Aunts—Fiction. 3. Drug abuse—Fiction.
4. Talk shows—Fiction. 5. Resourcefulness—Fiction.
6. Minnesota—Fiction.]   I. Title.

PZ7.Q17 On 2002

[Fic]—dc21

00-065860

for dave

ONE NIGHT

What's the worst thing you've ever done?

Think hard. Be honest.

Drink? Drink and drive?

Spread dirt on a friend? Cheat on a test?

Lie about something? Lie about nothing?

Ever kick a dog?

Have you hated someone hard for no reason at all?

Or maybe you had reasons—skin color, clothes, or

That gold symbol hanging around her neck.

You can't get much lower than that.

Unless you're poor Kelly Ray.

Poor, beautiful, lost Kelly Ray.

Nineteen now and just holding it together.

Nineteen and fighting to stay sober and clean.

Nineteen and trying, she's trying.

It's her second time clean, she's trying.

Yes, it's that old story, drugs.

Addicted so young, that old story.

But that's not the worst, that's not what has frozen her soul

And locked up her heart.

(Forgive me; it's her aunt Kit's rather ripe description.)

Poor Kelly—No, forget the poor. She'd say you should.

She'd say, Don't waste your pity on me.

She'd say, I did what I did, it's my life not yours.

She'd say, What you think and what you feel don't even reach me.

That's what she'd say, if she talked about it at all.

And what did she do that has frozen her soul and locked up her heart?

(I think I like Aunt Kit's description.)

What did she do? Okay, I'll tell, but hold tight because it's pretty bad.

Two years ago, when she was seventeen, detoxed and rehabbed

And clean for six months and trying . . .

Two years ago she took a fast slide . . .

Two years ago she . . .

Did I say that it's pretty bad?

Two years ago Kelly Ray nearly burned up her mother's new baby.

Still with me? I hope so. Because as awful as it is to think about—

Oh, God, yes, just think: sweet baby Louisa, five-month-old baby Louisa

Gasping for life in the smoke and the heat of the flames. Just Think.

Yes, it's awful.

But this isn't going to be a replay of nightmares,

Or a chance to crank up our cool

With an armchair cruise through dark places. No.

This, if not quite a fairy tale,

This, Reader, is a love story.

one

---

delivery girl

I bet ninety-five percent of all the female addicts in this town have really short hair. Buzz cuts, shocks, Marine mows, spike lids—whatever they're called, the Dakota City junkie/ex-junkie style is short. It's not like I'm noticing this for the first time or anything. I've just never thought about it. God, that's so true about everything, really. All the day–to–day crap, I'm only now clear enough to think about. This is sobriety, folks: the acuity to contemplate junkie hairstyles.

But still: the hair. Why short? Oh, nothing deep there, of course. First of all, it's The Look in this backwater town, and a big part of the user's fix comes from belonging, being part of The Scene. Fashion—any fashion—is all about the herd mentality, and why should it be different for dopers?

And then, too, who wants to bother with hair when you're only ever thinking of getting high, planning the how, when, and where of the next time? And especially why bother when sugar–voiced Julio down at Utopia Spa will pay twenty–five or more for even a short fist of dull

brown hair. Or if you're lucky like me and your hair is—
was—shoulder-length golden sun-streaked country club
blonde (yes, it's natural, Julio, can't you tell?), then you get
more. Seventy-five cash, or maybe you'd prefer—wink,
wink—some very nice product?

Sure, Julio, keep the cash. I'll just take a few bags of
that, uh, conditioning powder.

Okay, so it's clear why all the users go short, but why
oh why when we get clean do we all stay that way? I
mean, look at the women at this meeting. All of us no
longer using, but holding on and moving on, yet nearly
everyone here still looks like she belongs to a coven of
religious penitents, maybe one of those groups that—

"What is going on in your head? Did you listen to anything anyone said today?"

I lifted the head in question and locked stares with a
stern middle-aged woman. A stern middle-aged woman
with a salt-and-pepper spike lid. Wendi? Bambi? No,
Sandi, as in: Hi, I'm Sandi Q, and I'm cross-addicted. "Hey,
Sandi," I said. "Meeting over?"

"You'd know if you'd listen. You never listen. Never listen, never talk. Every day I see you come in here, take a
chair close to the exit, drop your head, and sink into
some daydream riff. About as involved with your sur-
roundings as a statue. Yes, the meeting's over, and if you
don't mind we're hauling the chairs over to the big room.
One o'clock AA needs them all."

I rose and she pulled the chair away, snapping it together and tucking it under her arm. I looked down at the

foam cup in my hand. An inch of cold black coffee was left in it. I closed my eyes and drank it down.

Sandi's fingers drummed on the back of the chair. "A bunch of us are going to lunch. I don't suppose there's any reason to believe you might want to join us. Do I need to even tell you that you are and always have been welcome?"

Several people had gathered near the exit. It was the usual NA post–meeting mix: some people laughing, some finishing up the tears. Most of them young and smoking.

I turned to Sandi, who was old enough to be mother to almost everyone in the room. "I have to go to work."

She rolled her eyes. "A real loner, aren't you? Honey, no one stays sober by staying alone. I used to be like you. I'd come to meetings and never do much but warm a seat. I crashed—crashed hard and stayed down until I started to do the work."

"I have to *go* to work," I said.

She followed me to the trash. I could hear her snicker softly as I tossed the cup and it bounced off the rim onto the floor. I leaned over, picked it up, and carefully placed it in the basket.

"What is your story?" she said. "I just hope I'm here the day you give it up."

"I've told my story. I've talked during round robins."

"Name tag stuff, that's all. We know your name, we know you're a sniffer not a shooter, we know—"

"I have to go, Sandi."

"Oh, yes: And we know you work for your famous

aunt. What we don't know is why you're here every day when she's on the air. Why is that, Kelly? Have you lucked out and found a job that's no job at all?"

People were waving from the doorway. I tipped my head toward them. "Your friends are waiting for you."

"Your friends, too—if you'd allow. Just tell me the one thing, Kelly: If you're really the assistant to a big shot radio star, why aren't you at work when she's on the air?"

I drew a breath, then released it in a silent whistle. "Because when Kit Carpenter is on the air, she doesn't need anyone."

Sandi handed the folding chairs under her arm to a lanky guy who was collecting them onto a cart. "Oh, so she's that big? I guess that explains why she doesn't even need Simone Sanchez."

"What?"

She smiled. "Paying attention now?"

"What do you mean—no Simone Sanchez?"

She tilted her head and narrowed her eyes. "Kit Carpenter's assistant didn't know?"

"Didn't know what?"

Her eyes lightened, pleased with my interest. "I ride the bus, right? Same route, same bus, same driver. Every day. And every day Teddie, the driver, has a radio tuned to KLIP. I always take the seat right behind Teddie because it's the safest place, and on the midtown route, you just never know. Anyway, so I'm up front behind Teddie and her radio, and all week I hear the promos: Simone Sanchez, live on 'Kit Chat.' But guess what. On the bus this morning Teddie's of course listening to the radio and suddenly she's pounding the wheel and swearing. Apparently, there's no Simone Sanchez. Instead—and I have to tell you, she nearly drove the bus onto the sidewalk when she heard this—all Kit Carpenter's devoted listeners were going to get today is your aunt grilling some lame community college professor about Lakveria and the conference at the U. No explanation whatsoever about why everybody's favorite singer is not going to be on the show. 'Couldn't be with us' was all your aunt said."

Oh, Kit. I swore, practically sputtering.

Sandi smiled. "Not that I approve of such language, honey, but it's good to see you off the leash."

I said, "I have to go to work."

Kit Carpenter's assistant didn't know and Kit Carpenter's assistant was pissed. My aunt has one of the highest rated daytime radio talk shows in the country. She's a natural born talker with a voice that glides through the air. And while she may not need anyone when she's mesmerizing her millions of devoted listeners, she gets plenty of help before the On Air sign lights up, most of it from me. For weeks I'd been researching and prepping her for the Sanchez interview.

Sanchez is a Diva Deluxe. So is my aunt. Who called whom to cancel?

I had my suspicions.

Normally it doesn't take me long to go from the meeting to work. It's a quick ten–block walk from St. Ambrose's Open Life Church down Washburn, then through the Medical Arts parking ramp to the unmarked staff entrance of the nation's biggest AM radio station, KLIP, where my aunt reigns and ruins. If the NA meeting runs long or the weather is bad, I can hop a bus, but usually I like the walk. And, as I said, usually it doesn't take long.

Unless you're dressed the way I was dressed today. Specifically, we're talking shoes.

I dress with care. This is not a fashion statement, or a declaration of class warfare. It's not even (I try to believe) the residue of once owning too many Barbie dolls.

It's control. There are a few simple road rules for life in the recovery lane. One of the biggies: Control what you can control. My options aren't many, but I can control how I look, so each day I present to the world a visually coordinated me. This doesn't always involve sensible shoes made for sprinting ten city blocks.

Today I was wearing some butter-soft Italian leather sandals. I can't buy these things on my salary, of course. I'd found them in my aunt's closet when I was hunting for scarves to braid into a belt for the red linen sheath I was wearing. I found the scarves—Paris silk; my aunt is nuts about such things—and I found the shoes. Help yourself, Kelly Ray.

The sandals were gorgeous but flimsy, not meant for movement more energetic than a quick stroll down a carpeted couture runway. By Washburn and Eleventh the toe loop on the left one had popped loose. By Eighth Street the right sole had split and was flapping loudly every time I took a step. By the time I reached the park-ing ramp, the other toe loop was loose, and every fourth step one or the other of the sandals would fly off.

A reasonable person might ask: Why not go barefoot? And a more reasonable person might answer: Not on your life. Not on city sidewalks three days into a swelter-ing heat wave.

Controlling what I could, I flapped and shuffled onto the ramp. The attendant glared at me as I ignored the No Pedestrians sign and walked up the down driveway toward the station door. Nothing unusual about that—she always glares at me when I ignore the sign and take the shortcut. But today she rapped on the window of her booth and shook her fist. I was about to wave her off when she stepped out and shouted, "Tell your aunt we don't need any more of the asshole professors. Where was Simone?"

I stared a moment, my jaw dropped open in imitation of the village idiot, then shrugged.

Miller, the KLIP security guard, also wouldn't let me pass without comment. Of course, he always has some-thing to say about nothing. He came out of his booth, stepped in front of the heavy gray door, and crossed his arms on his chest. "Kelly," he said.

"Hello, Miller," I replied. "Are you going to let me go to work? Or do I have to use the front door like the tour groups?" I looked down at my two dirty feet. "Please don't make me go in the other way."

"Kelly," he repeated.

"Miller," said I.

He narrowed his eyes and shook his head. "Would you please relay to your aunt the depth of my disappointment because today, contrary to what I'd been told, there was no Simone Sanchez to walk through this door and brighten the morning for a poor working slob. Instead I get to hold it open for a very angry station manager and a very livid president of programming." A slight smile spread as he watched me. "That's right, both about twenty minutes ago." He uncrossed his arms and motioned with his index finger. "C'mon, where is it? You know the rules, sweetheart. They're sitting in central security watching everything that comes across on that camera, so please help me do my job by wearing the badge where they can see it." He hummed softly as I pulled my wallet out of a pocket and fished out the ID. "Oh look at that," he said. "You're still holding only a temporary ID. Well, I don't suppose there's any hope of that changing now."

I slipped the wallet back into my pocket. "What do you mean, Miller?"

He shrugged. "After today's stunt, management will have to do something. Kit's untouchable, but the people around her might not be."

"Thanks, Miller. Thanks a lot."

"You've been warned, sweetie."

The very angry station manager and the very livid president of programming were going at it right outside the elevator door. Tyler McCall, my aunt's producer, was backed up against the wall. Obviously they couldn't get at the real target, so they were spitting at him instead.

"She locked the door again?" I asked as (barefoot at last) I stepped out of the plushly carpeted elevator and walked around them.

"You—" said one angry man.

"You tell her—" said the other angry man.

Tyler leaned limply against the wall and said nothing.

I didn't slow to hear what I was supposed to tell her, because after all, my aunt paid my salary, not the station, and I only wanted to hear what she had to say.

The two bosses followed me down the hall to Kit's office suite and stood breathing down my neck as I fished in my bag for the keys. The lock clicked free, the knob turned in my hand, and then I felt them start to push past me. "Gentlemen," I said. "It's in her contract; you have to be invited."

Yow, how those boys can curse.

Raoul, the station manager, added something else: "Goddam junkie gofer."

I beg your pardon: ex–junkie gofer.

The first time I remember seeing my aunt Kit was at my grandfather's burial when I was five years old. I was standing at my mother's side, her hand clenched hard around mine, when I unglued my eyes from the long, shining coffin and looked up as the crowd shifted slightly, opening up, everyone turning. All that morning people at the house had been talking about my father and whether he'd show for the funeral; after all, the dead man was his father. After hearing all the talk, I was wondering the same thing because I had never seen him. But it wasn't my father who caused the rustle, just a tall woman at the back of the crowd. The others whispered a bit, then returned their attention to the casket and the words being said. I kept my eyes on the woman, though. She was staring straight at me, and without her glance wavering a moment she produced a cigarette pack, tapped it, then removed a cigarette and placed it in her mouth.

Who smokes at a waiting grave? Back then I was not the least bit aware of those kinds of rules; that was not the astounding thing to five–year–old me. No, what held and charmed me was that the woman did it all with a silver claw.

I found out after the burial that she was my father's older sister. My mother and I had been living with my father's parents, which when you think about it must have been a royal complication in family life, certainly one so twisted and tight, I'm still not able to understand it. Unless, of course, it wasn't complicated at all, unless it was something as simple as my grandparents saying to my flat–broke mother and me, Our son has screwed you over, but we will keep you safe. But probably it was more twisted than that, because not only did my father keep his distance from his parents, so did my aunt Kit. She hadn't visited her parents in years.

So I had never met her. Until the day of the burial I'd had no idea I had a one-armed aunt.

She wasn't born that way. Her left arm up to the elbow had been shot off. As she likes to tell it—no, wait, maybe not; she likes to tell it with lots of detail about the blood and pain, and to pepper the story start to finish with really raw language. Not surprising, I guess, that she tells it that way, because it happened when she was a war correspondent in Vietnam and was following some Marines on a small action that went wrong. She says the story should reflect the reality.

But it's her reality, not mine, so all I need to say is that she got it shot off in Vietnam when she was covering that war. And all I need to make clear is that I fell in love with my aunt the moment I laid eyes on that claw. It was the coolest thing I'd ever seen.

My office is the outer room of Kit's suite, which I suppose makes me half receptionist, half guard. Before I knocked on the door to her inner sanctum, I listened for the post-show warning sounds. I heard typing. Kit does eighty words a minute with claw and fingers, fifty one-handed, but today the tap-tapping seemed slower than normal, so I figured she was unwinding with solitaire. As I opened the door, her computer erupted into tinny cheers and she sat back looking pleased.

"What's going on?" I said.

"I just won Gaps, difficult level. Do you realize how hard that is?"

"Not what I meant."

She shoved a paper to the edge of the desk. "Here are some things I want you to check before Friday. And I'm having doubts about tomorrow. Do we really want another show on genetic engineering?"

"What about today's show, Kit? What happened? We spent days prepping for Simone Sanchez, and you dump her? When did you do this? Who knew? Not Tyler, that's obvious. You can't make a move like this without telling your producer. You can't."

She swiveled in her chair. "Those sons of bitches."

I stepped closer. "Did you dump her or did she cancel? Raoul and Jerry are outside, both of them madder than hell, so I'm guessing you dumped her."

"Those sons of bitches," she repeated.

"You dumped her. Oh, man. They have a right to be mad, Kit. Number one on the radio is nothing compared to number one in the movies. Her CDs make more in a week than your show brings in over a year. And you dumped her, for a community college professor who thinks he's an expert on the war in Lakveria? *Lakveria?* Did this really happen, Kit?"

"Your Lakveria research was excellent, Kelly. I was able to challenge him on several points. His area was the history, and I kept up. I owe you for that. Good stuff, you always find me good stuff. But I don't suppose you listened today, did you?"

"You dumped her to talk about a war no one cares about? Simone Sanchez?"

She spun her chair around and faced me, furious. "Simone Sanchez used to be a good singer, back before everything she recorded started sounding like soundtrack schlock. And have you seen her last movie? She spent most of it in a gorilla suit, harassing an ex-husband's new girlfriend. This is a woman I want to spend two hours with?"

"What did you tell her? What excuse did you give?"

Silence.

"Kit, Tyler's likely to get fired unless you cough up something. Who knows who his replacement will be, maybe someone you can't ignore and walk over."

"I told her assistant that there were some breaking developments at the peace conference."

"Are there?"

My aunt's chair twirled and she looked at the skyline where the university buildings spread out along the banks of the river. She pointed and said, "*Those* sons of bitches."

I sat on the corner of her desk and looked out the window with her. Half a mile away world leaders were posturing at a special forum, making fine speeches about peace—or the lack of it—in Eastern Europe, especially Lakveria, the latest hot spot. The world's most important men and women, and Kit had been denied access to each and every one.

"Maybe," I said softly, "just maybe when you had the former vice president on the show you shouldn't have asked if he was a virgin on his wedding night. Or that interview with the former secretary of state? Do you suppose she liked being asked if she had a weight problem as a child? All these questions on the air, need I remind you? With your usual millions of fans listening in. Do you just suppose it might have destroyed your credibility as a serious journalist?"

"He's just pissed about the tree. I know that's what it is. So petty. He blackballed me because of the stupid tree."

You would not think this pleasant Midwestern city was a hotbed of diplomacy. Agriculture conventions you would expect, but not international peace forums. However, Dakota City is the birthplace and home of one Allen Ripley, former vice president of the United States, former ambassador to India, and, most recently, the former UN High Commissioner of Human Rights. That last job pretty much wore him (or Mrs. High Commissioner) out, and two years ago he came home to a statesman's retirement, which apparently involves serious gardening, frequent dog-walking, and hosting summits at his alma mater, Dakota City U.

Everyone knows about his resume, of course. I happen to know the details of his retirement because this particular former vice president of the United States lives next door to Kit and me. I get along fine with him; whenever we meet out walking, we always chat. But he's at war with my aunt. What the world does not know: The high-flying diplomat does not get along with his neighbor. For two years they've been arguing over a diseased tree on her property next to his garage that she refuses to cut down. And of course, there was the wedding night question.

Kit snapped to attention, snapped her fingers. Her eyes were fierce. "I want to be back in there, Kelly. I *want* it." Then her eyes faded to middle distance, dreaming about the past, probably mucking about in some war-ravaged country. I've read her stuff, stories so clear, you can almost smell the explosives and gunfire and blood.

After twenty years of combat reporting she settled in Washington to cover the men and women who made those wars. Two Pulitzers, three best-selling books—she was as famous as the world leaders she covered. And a better talker. Her experience and wit soon earned her prime television exposure as a talking head. Before long she had multiple, lucrative offers to create her own current affairs show; everyone from PBS to MTV was in the chase to own a piece of Kit Carpenter, witty, war-seasoned, photogenic, one-armed Kit Carpenter.

She walked away from it all. Turned her back on the hot television lights, left the cast of the most important political theater in the world to start a radio show from the prairie. Like the veep, she turned her back on what she loved and came home to Minnesota. Came home to take care of me.

I want to be back in there. Guilt and gratitude began their familiar roiling. It's a combustible combination, I assure you. I stayed mute, knowing it would pass, likely the moment she opened her mouth.

Kit breathed deeply and brought herself back. She

leaned forward and said, "Sketch it out for me, hon. You do that so well. So clear–headed. Ironic, isn't it? Sketch it out and I'll figure out what to work on, what to fix." Then she barked the command familiar to millions: "Talk now."

I counted it off on my fingers, rippling them in the air. I loved doing this to her; it made up in part for the frequent little comments like the one about my clear–headedness. "One, you book Simone Sanchez to come on the show the day before her only Dakota City concert in two decades. Simone Sanchez finally comes back to the town where she got her start and you're the one who gets the face–to–face. Simone Sanchez, the number one money-maker for the big ugly media company that pays your salary.

"Two, without telling anyone, you dump the number one moneymaker to interview a small–time professor, hoping you can remind people that once upon a time you were a serious journalist."

She cleared her throat. "I didn't ask for motivation, Kelly, just the high points."

"You apparently give the guy the whole two hours be-cause you want to score some points with the people at-tending a dull conference. People who are probably not listening."

"I don't need your speculation, either."

"Three, you have royally ticked off the bosses."

Kit opened her eyes. "*Ticked* off? Oh, honey, ouch." She smiled. "What should we do?"

Under the heat of her cheerfully expectant gaze I dropped my head and looked down at my bare urchin feet.

"Nice dress," my aunt murmured, following my gaze. "New, isn't it? You know, I think I have some sandals that would be perfect—"

"Kit, what's next? You have to decide."

She thought a bit. "Simone Sanchez. We work on her and make her happy."

I nodded. "Be a peacemaker, just like the warlords meeting over at the university. And how do you plan to do this?"

She flipped and caught a pencil with her claw. "Oh, no, you're the one who did all the research on her, Kelly. That part's for you."

Dakota City is a small town. The numbers might add up to Big City, but don't let that fool you. Want proof? Three million people, but only one hotel ritzy enough for po-tentates and movie stars.

The Poppy Hotel was thick with thugs—swarming with security guys intent on protecting the leaders and diplo-mats of every nation on earth, or at least every nation that wanted to be seen as concerned about peace in yet another war-torn small country in Eastern Europe. The local police had set up a security check at the hotel, and, patiently, I went through metal detectors, smiled while they checked my name against a list, waited cheerfully while they placed a phone call to the room upstairs to verify a final time that I was expected. A pair of Dakota City cops was handling everything, but they were being watched by what had to be a multinational phalanx of dark suits.

Before they ran the wand over me, I handed over the bag I was carrying. Kit had told me not to bother with gift-wrapping. She'd warned me that I and anything I was carrying or even wearing would be subjected to maximum security. No lie. I was fine with the wand, the questions, the close and skeptical scrutiny of my wallet and KLIP ID. I didn't even squawk when they confiscated my cell phone, a cop explaining apologetically that all electronic devices that hadn't been pre-screened would have to be held until I returned from the twentieth floor. Fine. But I must have made a noise when they started in on the gift I was taking to Simone Sanchez, because suddenly all the dark-suited men stiffened and stepped close.

"It's a rare book," I said. "It's fragile."

The Dakota City cop looked it over and then handed it to his partner, who scanned it with a wand and riffled the pages.

"A kid's book?" she said.

"A rare kid's book," I replied. "Rare and expensive." Probably twice as expensive as it really should be, because the dealer had sniffed out my desperation.

"You're taking a kid's book to Simone Sanchez? A used one?" The cop shrugged, then handed the book over to the nearest dark-suited thug. Then it got passed around, and one by one they made a show of personally examining *Little Girl, Big River.*

After they finally handed back the book, two guards escorted me to the elevator in the center of the lobby. I balked. "When we called, her people said we should take the private elevator. They said to come up that way. I'm expected on that one."

Simultaneously they pointed at this elevator just as the door slid open. My escorts were twins: both tall, big, and mean-looking. Deciding I wasn't really in the mood for argument, I stepped into the elevator with them right behind. The one on my left did the buttons while the other one watched me. I hugged the gift bag.

Just as the door started to close, two well-dressed and very tan shoppers rushed toward the elevator, their Neiman Marcus bags banging against their legs. "Hold please," the man called while his companion popped her mouth open and closed in silent distress. One of my guards held up his hand, palm out, and said, "Sorry." Outside the elevator, yet another suit stepped into view, barring their entrance. The elevator door closed and we began the smooth ascent.

"How come they don't need an escort?" I asked.

No answer.

"Should I have put the book in a Neiman bag? Flashed cash? Worn different shoes?"

The guy on my left was watching me with mask-like disinterest. I widened my stare, daring him to look down past the tasteful, cleverly belted dress to my feet, now clad sensibly in a pair of gleaming white, never-used Nikes I'd found in my aunt's office.

His pal cleared his throat. "They were going to a different floor."

We reached the twentieth floor—the special floor—in seconds. The door opened and the thugs nudged me out. Not surprisingly, it was no ordinary hotel corridor with a long row of doors. This was penthouse country and there were only two doors: one to my left and one to my right. The thugs nudged me to the left, 20-B. I looked over my shoulder at 20-A, wondering who was staying there and why they merited this security. No doubt one of the powerbrokers arguing impotently about peace. Thug Number One nudged me yet again, trying to move me along. I stopped and faced the jerk. "Don't touch me," I said. "Don't ever touch me again."

During my first dance with heroin, every now and then I slept in dark places in a favorite park. This wasn't your stereotypical homeless junkie crash, a sorry public collapse at the edge of an OD. I had a home with my mother and stepfather, and more often than not I snorted and nodded in the pastel splendor of my own securely locked bedroom. But sometimes nature-loving me (admittedly, she's easily confused with impatient, craving, can't-wait-to-get-home me) preferred the park. And one time I woke up to find some walking grunting blob of body odor digging through my backpack-pillow with one hand while his other hand struggled to get under and up my sweatshirt. The guy was huge and no doubt loaded on something, maybe insanity, and was intent on both working me over and ripping me off.

I sat up, or as up as I could get with his giant paw pressed against me, and said, "Get off me now; I'm going to hurt you."

A rapist or a killer wouldn't have been dissuaded, but Bigfoot was. He ran, fast, something in my voice and eyes showing him I meant business. My growling voice and glow–in–the–dark violet eyes.

Or maybe it was simply the sharp point of the switch-blade attached to the charm bracelet on my left wrist.

The security guy nodded. "Sorry," he said.

I cradled the gift bag in my left arm and rubbed that bare wrist with my right hand. No one messed with me. Ever.

His pal had already knocked on 20–B. It swung open, and there she was: Simone Sanchez, the great lady herself, her world-famous face contorted by an award–winning scowl. Right behind her were two more dark suits, one male, one female, Jack and Jill bodyguards. Simone Sanchez looked at each of my escorts, then glared at me as she yanked me on the arm and pulled me in. She slammed the door, shutting them out, and said, "This had better be good; I was about to get a massage."

I've been doing this job for six months, ever since I was released from the halfway house and got permission to work unsupervised. Kit's show is a must for people grinding out publicity, and she gets the full range of guests. I've researched them all and met quite a few. Not much surprises me now, and even less interests me.

Simone Sanchez grabbed my interest on the spot. It wasn't because she's been famous for longer than I've been alive. And it wasn't because I'm generally interested in people who grab hold of their lives and change them, somehow morphing into something new, maybe turning Judy Podolski of Boise, Idaho, into Simone Sanchez, star of the world. And it sure wasn't because this big shot celebrity was nearly naked under a gaping robe, her well-publicized implanted breasts pointing here and there.

It was the skin. A tabloid headline rolled through my head: Film diva battles midlife acne; aliens blamed for outbreak.

Who knew? Movie makeup must really be magic.

But that's the reality of being an ex-junkie gofer: Everyone you meet gets reduced to something banal. The movie star with bad skin. The radio host with one arm. The retired vice president who goes nuts over sick trees. Even Meryl Streep. I'd always thought she was this serious older actress, but she did Kit's show when she was in town promoting a movie, and now I know that—

"Delivery Girl? Hello, Delivery Girl. *Wake up*, Delivery Girl."

The solid gold voice yanked me out of the daydream riff. I felt the bag in my hand and took a breath. "Ms. Sanchez, Kit Carpenter extends—"

"Oh, please, don't tell me she apologizes."

Okay, lady, I won't.

"I didn't miss a thing by sleeping late today, Delivery Girl. I don't need Kit Carpenter; she needs me."

A smart ex-junkie gofer would have agreed, handed the old book to the movie star, and gotten out of there. But I said, "No, she doesn't."

Honest, the suits behind her stiffened. I guess anything less than complete obsequiousness must be a threat. One even patted his suit coat. An automatic gesture, no doubt, but I wondered if maybe he would've pulled a gun if I'd actually insulted her, if I'd said something like, Hey, lady, ever hear of benzoyl peroxide?

Simone tapped my arm. Weird: She was all smiles. "So the delivery girl has brass balls, just like the lady she works for." The female suit leaned in and whispered in the star's ear. Her eyebrows shot up upon receiving whatever information was relayed. She tilted her head, then Jill Bodyguard whispered a second dose of dirt.

I knew what it was. Simone moved closer and her eyes searched mine.

Never fails. They always do it. Once anyone knows, they check it out. Are you clean? Are you high? The eyes don't lie. I suppose for the rest of my life people who know will check it out. And because I live with a woman who talks to the world for two hours a day, plenty of people know.

Simone stepped back. "Tell your aunt she needn't apologize. I admire those brass balls, in radio jocks or delivery girls. Besides, this way I got to have breakfast with my daughter and her friends before they ran off to your monster mall." She held out a hand. "My staff told me you were bringing me something."

I gave her the bag. Simone Sanchez unhooked her eyes from mine, reached in, and pulled out the book. She gasped. "Oh, my," she whispered. "Oh, my." Then she gathered her robe closed with one hand and clutched the book to her chest with the other. She turned and walked to the first chair she came to and dropped into it. "I don't have this one, not the first edition. I've found all the other firsts in the series, but not this one." She beckoned. Her people stepped aside, allowing me to approach. "How did you know I didn't have it? How did you know?"

"It was a safe bet. Apparently hardly anyone owns this one."

A man dressed in white entered the living area through a door. "Madame? Your massage?"

"Henri, look: *Little Girl, Big River,* a first edition. Now I have the entire series in first editions. All of them, Henri. I have them all."

He stepped to her side. "I loved that show. The pioneer girl, yes?"

Simone made a sharp noise. "That wretched television show." She looked at me. "These books helped me survive a miserable childhood in Boise. They're why I came to Minnesota when I ran away at sixteen." She gave me a very slow once-over. "But I just bet you know all about me, don't you, Delivery Girl?"

"Of course I don't, Ms. Sanchez. But it is my job to do research for my aunt, and I do dig deep to find any information that might be useful for her interviews. Most of it I file away up here." I tapped my head. "You never know what might be useful."

"And how did you know that I loved these books? How did you know that fact and know it was *useful*?"

"There's a very active local fan club for the books. Kit's had some of them on the show a couple of times. That's how I've learned about the books, especially this rare one. And they've done some name-dropping—famous people who like them, that sort of thing."

Simone set *Little Girl* on her lap and laid both hands on top of it. "I hear from those women; they send me their newsletters. So you're saying that Kit Carpenter dumps me but she's had them on more than once?"

I smiled. "She read the books as a girl. The women amuse her. And they weren't ever competing with a peace forum."

Simone looked at the book, now back in her hands, then looked at me. "I presume she wants to reschedule me."

"Yes, very much. I'm supposed to ask for tomorrow morning."

She shook her head. "Not the day of a show. She's missed her chance to have me in-studio, but I'll do a remote. Sooner, rather than later, I think." She shrugged. "We haven't sold out Phoenix. Before then." Her eyes narrowed. "Not that I need Kit Carpenter."

"Her producer will call your assistant." I searched my head file for the name. "Ms. Whittaker."

Simone thumbed toward Jill Bodyguard. "There's Ms. Whittaker; make the date."

I shook my head. "Sorry. I'm just the delivery girl."

Handing me over to Simone Sanchez must have been all that the security guards had needed to do, because they were gone and the hall was empty when I left 20–B. Simone urged me to take the private elevator from her suite to a rear exit, but I needed to reclaim my cell phone. So I said a polite thank you and good–bye and left the way I'd come, through the twentieth–floor lobby. I punched the Down button, then glanced at 20–A. I could've sworn I spotted a shadow shift in the peephole.

The elevators were taking their sweet time. One minute. Two. Three. I ticked off the seconds, then realized there was no sense in that. A watched pot never boils. A watched elevator never moves.

Waiting time is lousy time. Hard time. My body always starts moving, keeping itself busy, tapping a hard beat on the floor with my foot, and before I know it I've chewed a tag of skin off my lip and it's bleeding or I've worked a thread out of the hem of my shirt. And if I take a deep breath to slow it all down, my nostrils are tickled by memory.

Not a day goes by that I don't want it.

The shortest way back to work takes me right past Joe T's, breakfast all day and very good fifty–cent coffee. Joe

T's is like a lot of places I know that serve very good coffee. You can also usually cop there.

I decided to go the long way.

I glanced at my feet, stopped the tapping, and saw that a lace was untied. I bent down and automatically reworked the laces while my head searched through files: Where's an afternoon meeting? I could use a meeting. One of those two–a–day days. Must be the heat.

The elevator door glided open and, startled, I sprang up. In an instant I was smashed against the wall, two unfamiliar security men holding me in place. Behind them was a guy about my age, his eyes round with surprise.

I didn't struggle, just breathed deep and held tight. One man restrained me while the other frisked me, his hands quick, all business, though these thugs probably got their thrills from their business. "Let me go," I said, my voice recovered at last. "I'm legit. Check downstairs, they cleared me."

"Let her go," said the young man, but the thugs didn't stop. My eyes locked onto his for a moment before he looked away. A blush, for dog's sake. Because he'd been ignored by the heavies? Or wasn't he used to being stared at by a girl?

A hand stroked my back; fingers probed under my belt. The search was all business, but I still didn't like it and I bit back a scream. Focus, Kelly, I commanded myself. Focus on something else or before you know it you might take a swing, kick, or bite; then they'd really work on you. Focus. Who's the guy, the young guy? He has to be Mr. 20–A. Why are they doing this for him? Why does he rate this brutal security?

I looked him over again. Dark and handsome, wearing a gorgeous suit with a very dull tie. No doubt about it, someone else should buy him his ties. The guy was obviously dismayed—deep breaths, red face, hands curled into fists, lips pressed together. In spite of the suit and the old man's tie, he looked for all the world like a little boy getting mad. His displeasure chilled my panic and I immediately relaxed. And the moment I did, it hit. All the Lakveria research for Kit paid off.

He was the prince, the king–to–be. The only direct male heir to a throne just restored to the royal family who'd been kicked out after World War II by the communist takeover. Mikel? No, that's the playboy uncle, great–uncle. An old man, warming the throne until this one was ready. This one, kept out of sight, you hardly ever heard about him, what was his—yes, that's it. Tomas. Prince Tomas.

Oh, Kit, you should be here, I thought. You should have delivered the damn book yourself. You'd have these thugs by the nuts and an interview in the can before they knew what hit them.

His eyes again met mine, still frantic. His hand ran over his hair, which rolled back from his troubled face in smooth brown waves. "That's enough," he said softly. "She's harmless."

Harmless. I laughed and the thugs paused. I said

calmly, "I'm sorry I startled you. I was tying my shoe and was surprised when the elevator opened. That's why I jumped."

No response.

"You can check downstairs. They know I'm here."

The prince spoke sharply in some strange-to-me language and then his men let me go. One whipped out a phone and punched numbers. Okay, now I know what's rule number one for a king-in-training: If you want to be obeyed, use the native tongue to command.

The prince seemed tongue-tied, exhausted by the effort it took to finally get his men to do what he wanted. So, keep talking, Kelly. "I delivered a package to Simone Sanchez. The actress? She's in Twenty-B. You can check with her. I'm just a delivery girl."

The one with the phone must have heard the same thing. He said something to his boss and nodded when the prince again spoke sharply. Then both thugs stepped back and assumed the basic bodyguard pose: legs spread, arms behind the back. The prince stepped forward. "I'm sorry," he said. "They're supposed to protect me, and you looked like . . . danger."

After six months of working for Kit I've learned to dig up piles of information. Okay, I missed the stuff about Simone's bad skin, but I don't miss much. I could tell you the history of this guy's wretched country and I could draw his family tree. I could give you the shopping list of atrocities carried out by all sides in the war—Laks and

Mernots, Christian and Muslim—and state the official reasons the royal family was invited back by the Lakverian Parliament. I could detail the UN's proposed peacekeeping plans and explain why the US Congress was holding back promised financial support. Pressed, with maybe a moment and no bodyguards glaring at me, I could even tell you where this guy's parents were buried.

But I had no idea why Prince Tomas Teronovich of Lakveria sounded like a Texan.

"It's not okay to have your men treat people like that," I said, "but we'll drop it."

"Thank you."

"Do you have to apologize for them often?"

He smiled and started to answer but stopped when a thug cleared his throat and rolled his shoulders. Evidently the bodyguards protected more than physical safety; indiscretion was also the enemy.

The prince rerouted his thoughts while he smoothed his awful tie and absently patted down his pockets. As he moved, a lovely scent fluttered in the air. Something familiar, what was it?

He said, "Did you actually meet Simone Sanchez when you made your delivery? She's there now?"

The elevator had closed and returned to the main floor. My hand hovered over the Down button a moment, then I let it drop. Tilted my head and looked at the guy. His Royal Highness was dead serious, earnest as could be, an eager boy waiting for an answer. Hardly a mile away grown-ups with real power were gambling with the future of his country while he wanted to know about a movie star. "I'm sorry," he said. "You probably can't say, can you?"

I drew a breath as I thought how to answer. Oh, man, *what* was that scent? Way too subtle for cologne. Lotion? Soap? Warning buzzers went off in my brain and I exhaled to quiet them (and rid my system of the mysterious fragrance). Pay attention, Kelly, the buzzer said. You have the crown prince of Lakveria waiting for you, an ex-junkie gofer, to say something. Don't be thinking about his pretty smell.

"Simone was there," I said.

His head whipped around so he could look at 20-B. He furrowed his brow and stared. I memorized it all, this snapshot of a prince mustering his nerve to make a royal decision.

Day after day, hour to hour, moment to moment, I expend most of my energy fighting one strong, life-threatening desire, and the surest way to win that struggle is to beat back all longing. But it roiled in me now, the longing. I wanted something, wanted it bad. I wanted *him.* I had to have him.

Whoa. Let me clarify. I wanted him, yes, but—cute as he was—not for me. No, I wanted to wrap him up, haul him out, and deliver him to Kit. Here, Auntie, the future king of Lakveria. The shining hope of a troubled nation. Tomorrow's show has a guest. Holy rap, wouldn't she have fun with this tender one? I could almost hear the first question, one that was really no question at all: *You, a king?*

Sometimes big decisions are made with no decision at all. The very first time I snorted dope it was like that. I'd just joined the house band at Poetry Haven. We played little jazzy interludes between readings, something to fill the air while the poets nerved themselves or fumbled with notebooks, or cleared their heads before speaking. The night in question had been an extra-long session because a vanload of kids from a writing camp at the university had descended on the Haven and they were all sharing their stuff. When the last reader produced a fat sheaf and launched into what promised to be an epic, I quietly unplugged my violin, tucked it under my arm, and followed Jake (keyboard) and Celeste (percussion) off the stage and out the back door. The Haven was on the second floor of an old warehouse in the riverfront district, and the back door only led to a small balcony overlooking the Dakota River. We closed the door on the smoke and poetry and started laughing about how screwed up writers were. The next thing you know, the powder came out. When it was my turn, I didn't say no because the question wasn't even asked. Of course, plenty had gone on in my life to bring me to that place, but at *that moment*, with something so huge in the balance, there was no decision to be made at all. Without even thinking or pausing or acknowledging any alarms going off in my head, I simply took the next step.

*   *   *

"Simone was there," I repeated. Then without even think-ing, added, "Do you want to meet her?" I didn't wait for an answer, just grabbed his arm to lead him along. Before his men could jump, I was knocking on 20–B.

Ms. Whittaker opened the door. How long since I'd left? Ten minutes? Five? I knew I had to move fast before anyone realized I shouldn't be moving at all. I said cheer-ily, "I know Ms. Sanchez was headed toward a massage, but this gentleman would like to meet her." I walked right in and pulled him along.

The assistant stepped back, allowing it all. "I'm glad you're still here, because Simone had a question."

I whispered in her ear. "His bodyguards are very jumpy; they worked me over in the hall."

She blocked their entrance. "Ms. Sanchez and her guests require no extra security. Please wait outside." A lady thug, but still a thug, and one of their own. They nodded respectfully and backed off. She closed the door.

I took a deep breath. Step one accomplished: I had the prince. Help me, Kit—what happens next?

Simone was still in the chair reading *Little Girl*. She looked up. "Oh, good," she said. "It's you. Maybe you know and can—"

I gambled and interrupted. "This is your neighbor, from Twenty–A. We met at the elevator. He wanted to meet you."

Simone set down the book, rose, secured the cord of her robe, and held the stage with a single slow inhalation.

Then, while we waited, she breathed out. Finally she said, "Well, goddam, it's the prince. So you're the reason my daughter and her friends couldn't have that suite."

He stepped forward, brushing right past me. Again, that scent. Must be a lotion. "I'm sorry we butted in like this, Ms. Sanchez. And I'm sure sorry your daughter couldn't have the room. I didn't know. I just go where they put me."

Simone briefly glanced at me, eyes widened, telegraphing as if to say: "A prince? You've got to be kidding." I pulled on a mask.

She gave him a sweet smile and waved away his apology. "It doesn't matter, really. She and her friends prefer the distance from me because they think then I won't notice how often they order from room service. So tell me, Prince: How's the peacemaking?"

"Not going well, ma'am."

"Oh, dear, is that really a politic answer? How come you're not shut up with the players?"

"It goes on without me."

"So you skipped out and grabbed the chance to meet a movie star. You're a fan, then?"

"My sister is a fan."

She made a little noise. Disbelief. "Your sister. Right."

I scanned the head files. Sister? What did I know? Yes, there it was: an older sister. Something else, something recent . . . The files flipped too fast, I couldn't find it.

"She's in the hospital," he said.

"How awful," Simone replied briskly. "I'll autograph a

picture for your sister the fan." She snapped fingers and people moved.

"No, thank you," he said. Some steel in his voice stopped the action. This was new, I thought. And it wasn't just his voice: He stiffened, stood taller, found the royal backbone. Even the tie looked better. "A photo wouldn't mean a thing," he said. "She's blind now."

We all froze.

"She's been a fan of your music for a long time," he said, "and now I can tell her that I met you. That's all I wanted. Thanks for your time." Prince Tomas made a slight, gracious bow to Simone, then turned to leave.

Think fast, Kelly Ray, or Kit's chance for an interview walks back into the arms of his thugs. I touched his arm. "Did I read that she's in a Paris hospital?"

His eyes rested on mine. "Yes," he said, coolly. I dropped my hand.

Simone stepped into our space. She looked at him (looking at me) and then looked at me (looking at him). This time, however, I could tell she wasn't checking for drugs as she locked onto my eyes. She was reading my mind. A hint of a smile, then she turned to the prince and hooked her arm into his. She said, "You can't possibly leave, young man; I want to hear all about your sister."

It was the weirdest thing: For a brief while he'd been able to be the prince—regal, gracious, poised, and cool—but now he was melting, a boy near tears. Simone and I saw it at the same time; she knew what to do. She gently guided him toward a chair and said, "No, I have a better idea. We'll have tea and then talk about her. And while they prepare it, tell me this: Why do you sound like a Texan?"

After a moment he reclaimed his composure. "My mother's second husband was a Fort Worth business man. We moved there when I was two. They divorced after a few years, but by then I was in a good school, and she . . . wasn't settled. So I stayed in Texas until I was ready for college."

I must have read that. I'm sure I'd known that. I should have remembered it.

He turned to me. I was standing behind the chairs, keeping a proper distance for an ex–junkie gofer. "How did you know she'd been moved to Paris? That wasn't widely reported."

"It's my job to know things," I said. "I'm a—"

"Delivery girl," Simone Sanchez blurted. She sprang up and pulled a chair over for me, motioning me to sit. "She found and delivered the loveliest rare book for me. What with all the important people in the hotel, they don't let just anyone in. I'm sure her . . . agency has her well–primed on anything and anyone." She sat back down just as Ms. Whittaker brought the tea service from a back room of the suite. Simone poured, regally. First she served the prince, then me. Her very bland expression as she handed me the cup was eloquent. It said: Shut up, Delivery Girl. If you want him, proceed with care.

I said, "Thank you, Ms. Sanchez."

She fixed her eyes on the prince. "If it's not too disturbing, would you tell me now about your sister?"

This time he wasn't ambushed. He was ready. "She was accompanying Red Cross workers while they delivered supplies to refugee camps. They were attacked on the road. Three of the workers were killed. Two survived, but barely."

"When was this?" Simone asked.

"Six months ago."

"And she's still in the hospital?"

"She was hurt pretty badly. That's why she was transported to Paris. That, and for her safety."

Simone looked up sharply. "Her safety? She was targeted?"

He nodded. "My sister was well known and popular in Lakveria. She'd been working with the Red Cross and various UN agencies for some time. There are . . . factions who are threatened by the stability the new government offers. My family, what there is of it, is part of that government."

"What about your safety, Prince?" she asked.

He sipped, swallowed, stared at his teacup before finally looking directly at Simone. "I'm well protected."

I must have made a noise, because they both looked at me. I smiled. "Lakverian security seems to be very efficient," I said. At least in hotels.

"What's your sister's prognosis?" Simone asked softly.

"Not good. She's alive and stable, but what she faces . . .

She lost her vision. Her left leg was blown off." He gripped his knee. "Severe internal injuries. Brain damage. She can't speak. There's partial paralysis, though the doctors have no idea if that and her speech loss are permanent." He set down his cup. "She responds to very little, though she seems to recognize some voices. She knows mine, I'm certain of that. We can't determine what, how much, she thinks. What she feels." He shrugged and looked down a moment, then across at Simone. "She can't read, can't communicate, she doesn't even seem to be there when I talk to her or read to her. So a lot of the time when I'm with her, I just play music. Often it's your music because I know how she loved it. And I can tell by the way she tightens her . . ."

He was no longer speaking to us. Just talking, just thinking aloud about his sister.

He breathed deeply. "Sometimes she squeezes my hand—sometimes she can do that much. Then I know that she's . . . there." He sat back. "She always loved your second CD. The one you recorded live at some college. It's just you and a piano."

Simone nodded. *"Simone Live,"* she said softly. "Oh my goodness, that's so old."

He said, "I play that and sit with her, whenever I can."

Simone made a tent with her hands. Tapped her fingers together three times, then smiled, her own composure regained. "I have a new CD, Prince Tom. I'll send it along with you. Though it's a far cry from *Live*. Raucous, that's what I am now, I'm raucous. Probably she won't like it. No, better you take home something else for her. Peace, perhaps. Yes, take home peace. But, oh dear, you say it's not going well."

"It's not. There's an agreement, of course. It's been in place for weeks. But we need more UN troops to monitor the cease-fire, and that depends on US money, I'm afraid. Congress is reluctant."

"UN forces didn't help much in Bosnia," I offered. "Nothing really did until the people voted and threw out the bad guy."

"Lakveria's different," he said. "We've had a bitter war, but no all-powerful evil leader. And all sides agreed in advance to honor the election. The fact that the parliament and the people voted to restore the monarchy shows that they want to find something to unite us."

"So you're to be a unifying force?" Simone said, a tad skeptically.

"Yes," he said firmly. "Exactly." He licked his lips. "Natalia, my sister, was working so hard. She knows Lakveria. She chose to live there years ago, when I was still at school. She . . ." He melted back into himself. "She should be the one. She should be the king." He looked up, smiling wanly at each of us. "Or queen." He sat erect in his chair. "But it's my job and I want it, I want to lead my country."

Simone twisted in her seat to pour more tea into her cup. She caught my eye and again telegraphed a message: Like hell he does.

The boy was no dolt. "I mean it," he said, leaning forward. "The opportunity is there now and it might not be

43

there again. We're hopeful. Six months ago this conference wouldn't have been possible. Your vice president Ripley has been very determined."

Determined to get a tree cut down, I thought, but that isn't going to happen.

"You're pretty far from Lakveria, but Minnesota is a peaceful place, probably a good place to conjure up peace," Simone said. "A very long time ago I lived here when I was just starting out. Sang in public for the first time in some divey beer joint near the university. Tony's Pub."

Not so divey anymore: Tony's was the most active jazz place in town, and they probably sold more five-hundred-dollar bottles of wine than beer.

And then it stretched before me: Step two, or how to turn him over to Kit. Tricky, though; I mean, I couldn't just suggest we all hop in the movie star's limo and take a trip down memory lane while the prince takes notes to share with his sister. Could I?

Prince Tomas rose. "Thank you," he said. "I must go."

"When we first got here, you said you had a question for me," I blurted, claiming Simone's attention. A rude commoner's interruption, but I was desperate and counting on the prince's good manners. He wouldn't dare leave until she bid him good-bye.

Simone clapped her hands together. "Of course!" She swiveled in her chair and reached for *Little Girl*. She opened the back cover and her index finger tapped the jacket flap. "Here, this: 'Ida May Turnbull lives in Dakota

City, Minnesota. This is her first book for children.'" Simone squinted at me, brow furrowed. "I know these books are about her childhood in Minnesota, but she lived in New York. She was part of the Algonquin round table. She died in New York. I've visited her grave."

"I guess she lived here before she lived there," I said.

Simone snorted. "Well, obviously. What I was hoping you might know—maybe those crazy book ladies told you—was where she lived when she lived here. Do you know? Is that fact in your head? If it's not, could you find out?"

If you focus on details, the big picture doesn't kill you. Details are my life preserver, one of the ways I keep afloat on sobriety sea. So, even though I have never read a single book by the long–dead Ida May Turnbull, I had done my research. And what I had missed, the ladies on Kit's show had filled in. Curse or blessing, I remembered it all. I said, "I know."

Simone Sanchez turned to Prince Tomas. "Helluva delivery girl," she said.

I thought he'd be confused, but he was nodding. "*Little Girl, Big River*," he said. "I used to watch the show."

Simone made a face. "The *show* was wretched. They should never make television shows from books. Never. The *books* are wonderful. You should read them, Prince. Read them to your sister. Tell her I insist." She turned to her assistant, still lurking discreetly. "Do we have time tomorrow to drive by this house?"

Ms. Whittaker shook her head.

Simone rose abruptly. "Show day; of course not." She pointed at Tomas. "You'll come to the concert, then you can tell your sister you heard me sing." She tipped her head to include me. "I've got tickets for the two of you. Pam, do we have those tickets?"

Oh, but the gears of stardom are oiled and smooth. In an instant, Ms. Whittaker flipped open a date book, pulled out two cardboard rectangles, and put them in the star's waiting palm. Simone pressed them into mine. "Call it a date or don't, but I expect you both there."

He was smooth. Not even a blush. "I'd be happy to call it a date, assuming I find out her name. But I can't attend. I'll be in New York. My uncle is speaking to the UN General Assembly tomorrow evening."

Hmm, and what was my excuse? I didn't have one, certainly not the UN, so I slipped the tickets into my wallet before they were reclaimed.

"Then if you can't go to the show, you must ride along now."

Ride along now? I wasn't the only one confused. "What?" said Prince Tomas.

"Ride along when we go to see the house of this author I love." She took a deep breath and moved in closer to him. Right before my eyes, the prince melted back into a boy. He gulped and licked his lips as she closed the space between them. Hard, I suppose, not to be aware of what was and wasn't there under her robe. "I just bet," Simone said, "that you know something about miserable childhoods, Prince Tom. I had one. Name the dysfunction,

46

any one you can think of, and I assure you that it was part of my family life. Reading kept me alive. Kept me sane." She held *Little Girl* aloft. "These books especially. I want to see where this one was written. So why don't you ride along? Something to tell your sister."

He stepped back. Took a moment. Rolled the thought around, clearly savoring it. Then he sighed and said, "Thank you, but I could never get away."

It's my job to be helpful, so I said, "Sneak out."

"My . . . men wouldn't allow that. They control everything." He looked to Simone for affirmation, one guarded person to another. But she was smiling.

"I almost hate to tell you this, Prince Tom, because it smells of one-upsmanship, but, dear boy, this suite is nicer than yours: It has a private elevator. You must ask for this room the next time you're in town making peace. So you see, your men don't even need to know that you've left. Fifteen minutes after we're gone, one of my people will step outside and say, 'Oops, did we forget to let you know?' "

"I can't go out," he said weakly.

"You're out now," I said, and gave him a moment to digest that fact before tossing him another. "And my name is Kelly Ray."

Simone insisted on sitting by a window *and* the prince, which meant the poor guy was stuck in the middle. I nestled into my corner of the backseat, right behind the driver, and tried to give Prince Tom room. He sat with his hands folded, looking down, looking inside, looking like someone trapped at a meeting in some musty church basement.

"What's funny?" he asked me tersely.

"Who's laughing?"

"You were, sort of. Under your breath. What's the joke, Kelly Ray?"

"No joke. It's just that sitting there the way you are kind of reminded me of someone."

"Who's that?"

"No one you know, Prince Tomas."

"Would you two please quit growling at each other," Simone said. "I want to enjoy this."

"There's a dinner at eight," he said. "It's nearly five now. I shouldn't have done this."

"You'll be back," she said.

Not if I get lucky, I thought. "No one made you come," I said aloud.

He looked at me a long time. Finally he said drily, "Is that what you think?"

Simone laughed and poked him in the gut. Then she looked out the window and said, "Are we there yet?"

Truth time: In spite of the enviable size of my mental database, I didn't know the exact address of the house we were off to see, just the general area. I was sure I could get us within a block or two and was counting on my memory of the rapturous description I'd heard from the Ida May Turnbull fans: corner house, red tile roof, brick and stucco, ancient hitching post out front. How many of those could there be?

"Head toward the U," I said to the driver. "Stay east of the interstate." He nodded.

Ms. Whittaker aimed and held a skeptical look. "No address?" she said.

I took a shot. "Fifth Street." She faced front and checked her watch.

Simone and Prince Tom were debating skiing in Switzerland versus New Zealand. He tried to include me, but I've never been east of Boston or west of San Francisco. I sure had nothing to say about restaurants in Gstaad, and the conversation rolled on without me. I watched traffic and wondered about Next.

Tell him outright what I want?

Keep lying about who and what I am until I can get Kit to meet us somewhere?

I reached into my pocket for my cell, then remembered it was still with hotel security. There was a phone on the back of the driver's seat. I asked, "May I make a call? I need to check in with my office and let them know what I'm up to."

"No," Prince Tom said in a tone that could command legions.

"This is a private excursion, Delivery Girl," Simone said gently.

"It will stay that way," I said. "I just wanted to check in." But I sat back. No sense upsetting anyone.

"I don't want this found out by the press," he said. "I'm supposed to be a participant in a serious conference. If it gets out how I really spent my time, it could blow things apart." He frowned. "But, Kelly, I guess maybe you should call, if you think you might get fired."

"Not likely," Simone murmured.

"Could happen," I lied.

He looked worried. "Could you call but not really tell them anything?"

"No," Simone said, stretching it into a two syllable word. Nuh-oh. "I don't want the press tracking us down either, Prince Tom. Journalists can be useful, of course, but then"—she smiled at me—"so are pesticides."

"Have you had your job long?" he asked me.

The way I figured it, talking about me would lead to one of two things: The lies would pile up or the truth would come out. Neither would help anything. I looked at the city streets gliding by. He waited. "Not long," I said finally. "Six months." Deflect, Kelly, deflect attention. "So tell me, Prince Tomas: Does your sister have a favorite Simone Sanchez song?" Might as well aim the spotlight where it was usually welcomed.

He folded his hands and nodded. "The Noël Coward thing."

Simone was watching me and she laughed. "Your head file finally fails you, Delivery Girl; you've never heard of Noël Coward."

I don't like being laughed at. To get even, I said, "That's a really old CD, of course; can you even remember the song, Simone? Can you still sing it?" My shot went wide; she wasn't touched. Maybe she'd been thinking the same thing.

Simone turned and looked out the window for a moment, then nestled down into the leather seat. She hummed a bit, softly, closed her eyes, and sang. "I believe . . ."

As she sang, sinking deeper and deeper into the slow, wistful ballad, I watched Prince Tom watching her. His eyes widened, he held still. He was memorizing everything.

Simone held the final note until it faded into a soft breath. She opened her eyes and said, "My, that was good! I haven't sung it in almost twenty years, and don't you think that was good? I should do those songs again. Pam, don't you think I should do all those songs again, just me and the piano, this time in the studio? Don't you think?"

Ms. Whittaker nodded.

Prince Tom whispered, "Thank you, Simone."

Then, oh my gosh, what a star move: She cupped his chin in her hand and pulled him over for a kiss.

I've seen a lot, of course, but this I could not bear to watch. I looked out the window. Just in time. "That's it!" I shouted. "There's the house!"

I'd never heard of Ida May Turnbull until I started researching for Kit. I wasn't much of a reader as a kid, and certainly never would have picked up anything hinting "historical." But I know now that this Turnbull, long dead, is one famous writer. Mostly because of the TV show based on the seven books in the Little Girl, Big River series. My grandmother didn't allow TV, so I never saw the show when I was little. And even though *Little Girl, Big River* is now one of those programs that's running in syndication somewhere every hour of the day, I still haven't seen it. Kit and I pretty much restrict TV to news and (if you must know) Hollywood biographies. Amazing, really, how many of those old-time stars had drug problems.

But evidently the Little Girl books themselves must be decent, because they drive so many people—women—nuts. Including, apparently, one very famous singing movie star.

Simone barely waited for the car to stop before she hopped out. "You're sure this is the place?"

Hitching post, red roof, brick and stucco. It checked out. "There should be a small metal plaque by the front door. Can you see one?"

She marched up to the house, climbed the steps, approached the door, then swooned before catching herself on the porch railing.

I said to Prince Tom, "It's the right house."

Simone knocked on the door, waited, knocked again. She turned to us in the car and shrugged, then hustled down the steps and walked between bushes up to a window.

"Oh, hell," said Ms. Whittaker, "she's off on a good one.

We won't be leaving here until she gets inside." She got out of the car, leaned against the hitching post, and pulled a pack of Camels out of her jacket. In a flash the driver was at her side and they both lit up.

Simone was moving from window to window, peering inside and no doubt leaving nose prints on the glass. "You'll tell your sister about this, I bet," I said to Prince Tom.

"Yes. Who knew? Look at her, like a kid. Funny, really, what strange passions any of us have."

Be bold, Kelly. The more you learn, the more ammo Kit will have when it's her turn with him. Besides, he's left a mile-wide opening. "What's your passion, Your Highness?" Either he had to think too hard or didn't want to say. Okay, then, soften the problem. "I mean, if you didn't have to be the ruler of a troubled country, what would you rather be doing?"

He ran a hand through his hair and leaned back, dropping his head against the cushy car seat. "Maps. I'd like to be back at Oxford studying maps."

Maps? He longed to cuddle up with maps? And they were counting on this guy to rule a country?

He must have seen something in my expression; he tensed. "It's not that comical, Kelly. Maps have it all: the history, philosophy, science, even the religion of a time and place."

"I don't think it's comical, Your Highness, I just—"

"Please don't call me that."

"What, then? You *are* a royal person."

Simone was back on the porch, knocking again. Loudly this time; we could hear the banging from the car.

"Prince Tomas—would you rather I call you that?"

He shook his head, then tipped it toward the house. "What she says: Prince Tom. I like that."

"Okay, Prince Tom. I don't think loving maps is comical. The answer was just so unexpected."

He repeated it softly: "Unexpected." An eyebrow arched. "All this is unexpected, wouldn't you say?"

An understatement, of course. I nodded. "I was just delivering a book."

"And I was returning to my room for a clean shirt."

I peeled my eyes away from his face and glanced down. "Your shirt looks fine." Sheer white, crisp, expensive, tailored perfectly over an obviously trim build.

He held the suit coat open wide, revealing a spot on the shirt. "Ketchup," he said. He smiled. "Now you tell me, Kelly Ray: What's your passion?"

Staying sober, I thought. I glanced away. "I don't have one."

"I bet you do."

I didn't suppose he'd like the idea of keeping company with a former addict, so it seemed to be time—again—for an alternate to the whole truth. "It used to be music, Prince Tom. Once upon a time I played the violin. I was very good, once, and I loved it. Did you know the Dakota City University has a famous map collection?"

During the time he silently looked at me, I swear his

eye color shifted from brown to green to brown again. "You changed the subject," he said softly.

"I know I changed the subject. You're the visitor in town and I wanted to know if you knew about the university collection."

"How do *you* know about the collection?"

"That's kind of insulting, Prince Tom. Do only map lovers know about map collections? I've lived here all my life. I hear things. I file them away."

My hand hadn't budged from my lap, but he sure looked as if I'd slapped him. "I didn't mean to say anything insulting, Kelly. You just surprised me. Maps aren't even on the radar for most people, so I'm always surprised when someone knows anything at all. I admit, though, I might not have perspective. You see, I don't simply like looking at maps. I had hoped to spend my life with them. Studying maps, teaching maps, writing about maps. So, yes, I know about the collection here. Did you know that it holds one of the most valuable maps in the world?"

"No, I didn't."

He nodded. Leaned closer, then laughed.

"The joke, Prince Tom?"

"You, sort of. Watching you work, I guess. You filed that nugget of information away, didn't you? Closed your eyes and put it somewhere in there." He gently tapped my head twice before letting his finger rest for a moment on my hair.

I watched him pull back and secure his hands in a

tight clasp. How long, I wondered, since he'd been free to touch a girl?

For that matter, how long since I'd touched a boy?

His eyes did the color thing again as he waited for my answer. So did his cheeks, actually. From pale to pink to pale again. I said, "I suppose I did file it."

"I wonder what else is in there."

"Lots of details, most of them useless. Hey, look at that."

A small crowd had gathered on the sidewalk and was watching Simone prowl around the house. I glanced at her driver and bodyguard; they seemed unconcerned. More likely they were hoping that the unsolicited attention would end the excursion.

A woman moved toward Simone. She held out a pen and paper. As the pack followed the autograph seeker, Ms. Whittaker, finally inspired to run interference, got off her perch and strode toward her boss.

"Simone's been discovered," I said.

From the safety of the car we watched her sign autographs and talk to strangers. She said something to her assistant, and then Ms. Whittaker headed back to the car. She opened the door, reached in, and dug into a bag on the front seat for a moment before pulling out a disposable camera. "She wants pictures. You two, out. She wants you in them."

The crowd was getting larger. Somehow word of the star's presence in the neighborhood was spreading. "No," Prince Tom said.

Ms. Whittaker swallowed and licked her lips. "She thought you'd say that. She said to tell you the photo will never be released, it's for her private scrapbook." She sighed heavily. "She's so into scrapbooks. She also said to tell you, Please." Prince Tom and I exchanged looks, shrugged, then got out of the car and walked to Simone, following Ms. Whittaker, who wedged a path through the giggling fans.

" . . . fabulous books," Simone was saying. "I want you all to promise to buy them and read them. And she wrote the first one right here. Right here! There you are, you two. Pam, take our picture." Then Simone was gripping us both by the elbows and guiding us onto the porch. "Everybody, you would not believe it! This is—"

"Don't, Simone," I muttered. "The spotlight stays on you." She looked at Prince Tom. He nodded and mouthed a word, *Please*. Today's magic word.

"These are my friends Tom and Kelly. Give us a minute to snap a picture, then we'll talk more." After the shot was taken, they swarmed around her. Prince Tom and I were edged aside.

A tall gray-haired woman reached out and grabbed Simone by the hand. "I live next door," she said. "The woman who owns this house just ran out to pick her daughter up at soccer. She'll be right back. I'm sure she'd be happy to let you in and see the house."

Simone swooned again.

"Oh, hell," Ms. Whittaker said. "Now we're really stuck."

Prince Tom looked worried. He turned toward the car,

glancing up and down the street. "The press will be here any minute," he said. "Surely someone's called by now."

"We can go," I said.

He chewed on his lip. "I never should have done this."

"We'll leave and no one will know."

He still wasn't hearing me. Probably running through in his head all the international implications of being on the lam with a swooning movie star. I tried once more. "Let's go see the maps," I said. "The campus isn't far. There's a new special collections archive that's supposed to be wonderful. Maybe they have your valuable map on display. We could be there in minutes."

Now I had him. "Really?"

"But we'd better go quick, before word gets out."

"I shouldn't."

"You shouldn't be here, either, but you did that."

"I don't know . . ."

"Make a decision, Prince Tom."

His eyes went cold. "All right, Kelly. Let's see the maps."

I pushed through the crowd to Simone. Hard to figure why she kept bodyguards, because the lady was loving the contact with the pickup audience, everyone apparently a devoted Simone Sanchez fan. I caught her eye. "We can't wait; we're leaving."

She patted the air around her, trying to back the people up. "Give me a minute, dear ones; I'll be right back."

She linked her arm through mine. "You don't want to go inside? I can't believe I get to go inside. You mean you don't want to?"

"He doesn't want to be caught by the press, Simone. So we're sneaking off to see—"

"Don't say, Delivery Girl. Then I can't tell if someone asks me." She held her arms out to the prince. "Wonderful boy, give my love to your sister. Tell her she's inspired me to record another CD like *Live*. Tell her she'll get the very first copy." A hug, kisses, then a grand sweeping turn back to the waiting crowd. Within seconds she had two wide-eyed fans in her arms and was preaching to them about reading.

Prince Tom and I hustled away. I checked over my shoulder. No one followed, no one looked.

"So what's this rare map you hope to see?" I asked. I wasn't really interested, but I wanted him to keep his mind off where he should be and what he should be doing. Keep him running, keep him happy, keep him busy until I could hand him over to Kit.

"It was made for Charlemagne. It was a map of his empire, engraved on a silver plate. Charlemagne's map, right here in Dakota City. We're taking the bus?"

"I'm a delivery girl, not a movie star, Prince Tom; this is my limo." I pushed him on board. He stared at the fare box. I paid for us both. He fell into a seat as the bus lurched. I slipped in beside him and smiled. Ancient maps he knew all about. Public transportation apparently was a mystery. How in the world could he ever rule a country?

As the bus rolled along, Prince Tom chatted about the map he hoped to see. I listened, sort of, while I thought about the university buildings, bus stops, and how to make sure we avoided the part of campus where they were holding the forum. If we got off at the student union and then took a campus shuttle ... I planned it out while he talked about Romans and Franks, cartography, roads, empire building. I heard some—enough.

Charlemagne: Now *there* was a king.

Bad news. When we got to the archives, the first thing we heard was that the one map Prince Tom most wanted to see was out of reach, couldn't be viewed, not available to anyone. All this—but no reason why—crisply relayed by a student sitting behind the reception desk at the map library. I tried reasoning with her. "This is a public university," I reminded her. "Everything's free and open to the public."

"Doesn't matter," she said.

"This place is empty," I said. "No one would know."

"No way," she said.

Prince Tom tried charm bordering on seduction. That was a better idea, because the student–on–duty was obviously bored with sitting on a hard stool at a desk and reading *Valley of the Dolls,* which was all she had been doing when we arrived. The two of them bantered for a while. She was melting, but, still, no go. She tossed her head and giggled. "I can't, I can't, I can't," she said. I swear I was about to shake her when Central Casting sent in a professor.

I mean, this guy was *it*: worn tweed jacket, pockets

bulging; tie askew; disheveled white hair; eyeglasses resting crookedly on his nose. And he wore red Converse sneakers.

The girl sat primly at her post. "Dr. Larson. I didn't expect you back after the seminar." She turned to Tom and me. "Dr. Larson is the curator of the map collection. He'll confirm what I've been saying."

The geezer looked us over. "Well?" he said.

Tom said, "Dr. Ralph Larson?"

Again: "Well?"

"I've heard a great deal about you, sir. I studied at Oxford under Bulworth Smythe-Warwick."

"The hell you did!" The old guy whipped up so sharp and erect, I expected to hear bones snap. "You're one of Bully's students? Well, as I live and breathe." He leaned forward and looked hard. "Not a Brit, are you?"

"Raised in Texas," Tom said. Truth as evasion; not a bad trick. He offered his hand. "Tom Buckhorn."

I didn't laugh, which was a huge accomplishment, but I did nearly gag on spit. Buckhorn? *Buckhorn*? Okay, I could understand why he wouldn't toss around Tomas Teronovich, but *Buckhorn*? Prince Tom turned slowly and stilled me with a regal stare.

On the other hand, if you've got to hide behind an alias, why not choose a manly one?

Professor Larson scanned Tom Buckhorn's slick suit. "Your accent says Texas, but I'm not sure your clothing does. Oh, that's probably my ignorance and prejudice. Either way, if you're one of Bully's students, you're smart as a whip, and that's all I ever care about. How may I help you, Tom?"

"My friend and I would love to see the Charlemagne."

"Can't."

Tom nodded, his face regretful. "That's what your aide told us. I suppose only a few researchers have access."

"They might get away with that at Oxford, but not here," Professor Larson said. "In the US of A a public school means public. Our collections are open to the tax-payers. And even if we did limit access, well, you can be sure I'd give the okay to one of Bully's boys."

"Then why can't we see it?"

"It's not here. Permanent loan to the Library of Congress. Hasn't been announced yet, but I delivered it my-self last week. Just missed, my boy. Sorry."

The prized map was gone, but the genial professor had other things he thought Bully's boy might want to see. Tom and Dr. Larson—both blithely accepting my claim that I needed to use the bathroom—disappeared together into the archives.

It wasn't the bathroom I wanted. I'd spotted a pay phone near the library's front door. I'm sure I could have cajoled Valley of the Dolls into letting me call for free from her desk or one of the offices; I mean, after all, I'd brought one of Bully's boys to delight the head man. But I didn't want her listening in, because I needed to call Kit and arrange the next move. Prince Tom might not be ready to talk and tape an interview, but I didn't know how much longer I could string him along. Better to let Kit at him now.

She didn't answer at home. Odd, because at this time she was usually planted in a favorite chair, drinking ginger ale, and keeping up a running commentary on the news programs. She didn't pick up at the office, either, and her cell phone threatened to ring on into infinity.

But the most puzzling thing was that there was no voice mail, not at even one of the numbers. I kept waiting for the familiar message: *This is Kit Carpenter. Talk now!* Nothing.

She always left a way for people to get in touch. Kit would die before she'd be out of touch. Okay, sometimes, if the show had been especially hot, her interviews or commentary especially provocative, she'd stay away from the office phone until things cooled down, until the guys at the station saw the ratings numbers and decided to can the "you can't do this sort of thing" tirades. But even on those days she kept the cell on and open. It was her private link to her private world. And only a few people had that number: a couple of friends from DC (*Kit, honey, I'm just back from the White House, and you would not believe . . .*), her personal shopper at Nordstrom (*I've got some fabulous new Eileen Fishers; you should see these jackets!*), the chef at D'Amicos (*The scallops are in, luv, and they're perfect today*).

And me. I had the number. *Kit, I'm at the U map library with the prince of Lakveria. He might be ready to talk with you. Shall we meet at the station and tape a segment for tomorrow?*

That was the message she didn't want to hear. Didn't dare hear. That must be it. The thugs wanted their prince back. They'd found out that he wasn't in the hotel room or with Simone, but they didn't know where he was now. Just that he was with me and that I worked for Kit. One way or another, they were keeping her company until they found me. So she'd shut me out and wasn't letting me call.

That meant one thing.

Kit knew what I was trying to do. They'd told her I was loose with the prince, and she knew what I was trying to do, knew I'd be in touch, knew they'd be on me in an instant if I checked in. She knew, and avoiding the phone connection was her signal: Go for it, Kelly. Bring him in, but you're on your own.

Valley of the Dolls was locking up when I returned. "Closing so soon?" I said. "Isn't it a bit early for the university library, even for summer session?"

"Not this area," she said. "Special collections all close at six. Your friend is back in the study room with Dr. Larson. It's the last door down that hall. Would you tell the professor that I've locked up and gone?"

There were several rectangular tables in the study room. Most were strewn with books and journals. Tom and his new pal were bent over a map laid out on the table farthest from the entrance. They were both wearing white gloves. Dr. Larson tapped the surface of the paper. "There it is! Do you see how she initialed it, working the letters into the illustration? E.R. Elizabeth Regina. Bully discovered that. Of course, he had his copy to contrast it with, and so this addition jumped right out." His expression saddened. "His copy has Drake's initials."

"I've studied it," said Tom.

"Lucky boy," whispered the professor.

I sat at a table across the room from them and started thumbing through an atlas while they continued to pore over maps. The professor said something, and Tom happily slapped his hands together in a soft clap. Good joke, I guess. Then Tom pointed at something and replied. The professor threw back his head and roared. Cartographer humor. What a riot.

They hauled out another map and continued their private jokefest; I began a mental list of notes and questions for Kit. Ask him about Oxford, maybe about this Bully. And what was it like going to school as a kid in Texas? Oh, yes: Skiing in Switzerland—how does that prepare you for leading a troubled country? And just how rich are you? The royal family supposedly drained the Lakverian treasury and emptied museums before it left on its fifty-year exile. Any plans to give some of it back? And one final question for you, Your Highness: What's so funny about maps?

Tom had taken off his jacket and draped it on the back of a chair. His shirttail was working its way out of his pants, his tie was pulled loose, and he'd rolled his sleeves up, exposing sinewy forearms above the gloves. He leaned forward to catch something Dr. Larson was saying, and the shirt tightened across his wide shoulders. His eyes stayed fixed on the professor while he listened, not wavering a moment. What would it be like, I wondered, to have those eyes pinned on me?

Their talking buzzed on. I put my head down on my arms. Okay, somehow I'd figure out what to do and how to deliver him to Kit. Nothing was urgent now. I'd gotten him this far. Out of sight and out of reach of his guards.

My eyes caught Tom's. He was watching me now, looking over the professor's bowed head while the older man studied something on the table. Just before I closed my eyes, we both smiled.

If I were any closer, I bet I could watch those eyes do their color switch. If I were any closer, I could breathe in that lovely scent. I could maybe even—

Whoa, Kelly Ray. Remember who you are and what he is.

You're a delivery girl. He's the package.

Prince Tom's hand touched my shoulder. Caressing, then slipping down and cupping my—

"Wake up, Kelly. Time to go." He shook my shoulder, the hand gripping unromantically hard. I came to from a deep sleep, wiping the drool off my chin before I raised my head. I sat up and looked around, remembering.

"You crashed hard."

How true, Your Highness. "Where's the professor?"

"Putting things away and calling his wife. He's invited us home for supper."

Oh, man. No way. Risking a run-in with the thugs waiting for me at Kit's would be better.

"I'd like to," Tom said. "He's so excited about it. He says he can't wait to introduce his wife to one of Bully's boys. He's been so kind, Kelly."

"Sounds great," I lied.

He looked puzzled. "You can't mean that. You don't have to come along, you know. I'll go back to the hotel after I've done this. I'll face the music and take the blame. I'll make sure it's all squared with your agency. You should go home; you're tired."

Fat chance, Buckhorn. Lose you now? Time for some truth. Half truth and full guilt. "Prince Tom, by now your people know who I am and they know where I live. I bet they're waiting there now. I can't go home until I know that you've showed up at the hotel and explained everything. You saw how they worked me over. Do you think I want to go home and face that?"

He paled.

Slow down, Kelly. Play it straight, but don't get him scared. "Besides, Tom, do you think I'd miss my one chance to have dinner with royalty?"

That earned a half smile. "Okay, then, we'll have dinner together. But tell me: What happened to *Prince* Tom?"

"Sorry."

"No, it's better. Just Tom, that's good." His eyebrows arched. "I saw you laughing when I told him my name."

"Buckhorn? You have to admit that you came up with a good one."

"It's for real. Well, used to be real."

How had I missed that in the research? He kept on smiling, waiting.

Light dawned. "The Texas stepfather?"

He nodded. "I'm not so sure that *he* didn't make it up, though; his background was a bit sketchy. But I was happy to use it, at least as long as I lived in Fort Worth. I don't think Teronovich would have gone over very well with the good ol' boys at Sam Houston Military."

Sam Houston Military—more background I'd missed. Everything before Oxford was a blank, really. There was probably plenty of material I should get out of him before Kit took over. Questions formed in my mind, but before I could start asking, Dr. Larson returned, looking unhappy. "I've done it again," he said.

Tom and I exchanged worried glances.

"I called my wife to warn her I was bringing guests. She wasn't there. Then I checked my voice mail. Apparently I've forgotten another dinner party, this time for my granddaughter's fifteenth birthday. I'd bring you two along, but Cassie wouldn't appreciate Grandpa's friends. Not at her age."

I gave Cassie a rousing, silent cheer.

"Could I drop you someplace?"

Before Tom could say "Poppy Hotel," I blurted, "Where do you live? What's on the way?"

"I'm headed over to my son's house near Lake Ethyl."

"Could you drop us in Midtown? We'll grab dinner there."

It pleased the man to do the favor. He hummed tune-lessly as he closed up the study room and led us out. As he fumbled with the lock—trying again and again to get it set—Tom pulled me aside. "I think I should go back to the hotel, Kelly. If he drops me off first, then you can go home and know that when you get there, it will be all clear. I assure you: You will not be bothered."

He was *not* getting away. "But what about dinner? I'm starved. You must be, too. I know some great restau-rants."

His head dipped, he sighed, his eyes wouldn't meet mine.

"Tom?"

He steeled himself with a deep breath, let it out with a slight whistle, then said, "I can't buy you dinner. I don't have any cash or plastic or anything with me. Hell, I hardly ever carry a wallet anymore."

There was something kind of sweet about his discom-fort. "Doesn't matter, Tom. My treat. You're the guest in town and I get to play hostess."

He shook his head. "It's not just the money, Kelly. The afternoon was wonderful, but I should return to the ho-tel. It's time."

"Time for what?" Dr. Larson said as he joined us.

"Time for dinner," I said to him. I turned back to His Royal Highness. "You promised, Buckhorn."

Dr. Larson dropped us off in the middle of Midtown, right in the heart of all the clubs, stores, and theaters.

Traffic stalled, horns blew, people screamed as his dented Toyota crept along Atwood Avenue, stopping unpredictably and often as he mentally measured then rejected possible pull-over spots. The good-hearted man was oblivious to the havoc he created. We finally convinced him to let us hop out at a red light. We hustled out, gained the safety of the sidewalk, and turned to wave good-bye. He leaned on his horn in response, then sped away, tires squealing.

Tom stared after him in wonder. "When I am the king," he said finally, "senior citizens will be respected, cared for, and each one will have a personal driver. When I am the king—"

I didn't hear what came next because my attention was diverted when a police cruiser passed. Slowly. The cop inside took a long, hard look at the two of us yakking it up on the corner of Atwood and Bovey. And why not? We'd just emerged from a car that had created the biggest neighborhood disturbance since the window-smashing and trash-bin emptying that occurred last August after the police closed the after-hours nude beach on Lake Carney. So, yes, that might have been the reason he was staring. On the other hand, he may have been alerted to watch for a spike-haired girl in a red dress and a tall prince in a dark suit.

The policeman was still looking. Once upon a time, cop stares scared me for a different reason. I was clean now, but I was keeping company with a fugitive prince. Time to get invisible.

I took Tom by the elbow and moved us along in the opposite direction of the cruiser.

"Where are we going?" he asked. "I'm starving."

I glanced over my shoulder. The cruiser was out of sight. "I think we've been spotted. I think the police are looking for you."

"I doubt it. The media would pick up on that. Don't they listen in to police radios? There's no way my uncle would risk that sort of publicity. His security people might be out looking, but not your police."

"Don't be silly, how could your watchdogs handle that sort of search? They're big and they're ugly, but they don't know their way around. They have to use the locals, Tom, and I'm sure that cop was looking at us for a reason. He's probably circling the block now, maybe calling us in. How badly do you want to have dinner before you're picked up and returned to the hotel for a royal spanking?"

He checked his watch. "Seven already? And what I face when I get back is worse than a spanking: There's the dinner at eight and then an evening of speeches. I want to eat, Kelly. I'm hungry. You hauled me here and now I want to eat. So what are you getting at?"

"Look at all the people, then look at yourself."

He obeyed, then shrugged. "I still don't see."

"Prince Tom, it's time to lose the suit. And it's way past time to get rid of the tie."

Midtown is the only neighborhood in Dakota City with any life. Everything mixes up here: The street kids call it home, artists and writers lounge in the coffee shops, cultures spill from the restaurants and blend on the sidewalks, musicians jam in parks and on street corners. Even the suburban mamas love it, coming in during daylight to patronize the urban hair salons. And in a hundred different places—corners and back rooms, alleys and apartments—dealers deal, users cop, addicts crash.

I don't spend as much time in Midtown as I used to.

The Midtown People's Center was on a side street at the edge of the neighborhood. Thanks to my previous life, I knew which alleys were too narrow for cars and which stores had back doors. I got us to the center without being spotted.

The food bank and clothing exchange were both doing brisk business. It was near the end of the month, which meant empty cupboards, and these first really hot days of summer meant even street people were shedding winter clothes.

"Is this stuff clean?" Tom asked as he poked through the hangers and piles of folded shirts.

"Perfectly clean. Just used."

He found some jeans, a T-shirt, and sandals, and went to a dressing room to change. While he was changing, I found some shorts and a shirt I'd probably have to possess even if I wasn't trying to evade the police: a powder blue T-shirt emblazoned with a portrait of Elvis.

When we met outside the changing stalls, I gasped, then laughed.

"What's funny?" he said, clearly not amused.

What could I say? Without the suit, he looked so young. The boy who would be king. "You look great," I said. The truest words I'd spoken all day.

He was pleased. He held up his clothes and the glossy shoes. "What about this stuff? Can we get a bag?"

"Leave it all, especially the suit. They'll clean it up and someone else can use it. Someone who needs it."

"It's custom-made."

"Then some laid-off, dead-broke dad will look terrific and feel confident when he puts it on for a job interview."

We dropped our discards in the donation bin and I deposited some cash in the Pay What You Can box at the front counter. The clerk looked up from folding shirts and nodded thanks.

There was a crowd outside the building. A sign advertised a free concert and people were gathering. In our discount duds, we blended in.

"What else goes on here?" Tom asked.

"Soup kitchen, literacy classes, twelve-step meetings, job training, you name it."

"Dakota City looks like such a healthy, wealthy place. All this is needed?"

We dodged a bus as we crossed the street, then stood still a moment to let a pack of skateboarders dodge us. "It's all needed very much," I said. "No city's ever that healthy. Do you have anything like it in Lakveria?"

"Refugee camps is what we have. There's a war going on, remember? The Red Cross runs them."

"Well then, Prince Tom, when there is peace and

when you are the king, you know what you can do to help."

He paused and looked back at the crowd outside the center. His eyes blinked as he studied it all. You could almost see the gears shifting, see the lights going on.

"They feed people here?" he asked.

"That's what the soup kitchen does."

"Health care?"

"A free clinic, open seven days a week. Whatever it is, if someone needs help, this is the place."

Tom nodded. "When I am the king."

We headed back to the heart of Midtown. I supposed it would have been smarter to go to some other neighborhood, but this was the only one with decent restaurants, and right now food was what mattered most. Tom wanted to eat Korean, I felt like Indian, we agreed on Thai. It was a good decision.

Tom pushed back from the table. "That was excellent."

"I ate like a pig," I said, then signaled the server. I wanted dessert.

We'd been given a window table and I was sitting with my back to it. Maybe this wasn't the best way to hide, but with our change of clothing we blended in. Besides, the parked cars and sidewalk traffic blocked us from cruising patrol cars. Still, I'd noticed how all through the meal Tom's eyes drifted to the outside. Either telling him about the cop had made him nervous or he was bored with me. Fifty-fifty, I figured.

We ordered some Thai cakes and tea. His eyes settled on me. "This is maybe an embarrassing thing to admit," he said, "but it's been one of the best days I've ever had. Simone Sanchez. The library. Evading your police and missing my boring dinner. This incredible meal."

"Life's not too exciting, then?"

"And being with you. That's been very nice."

"Definitely not exciting."

He smiled. "What's the best day you've ever had, Kelly?"

This I didn't want: questions. Always good with evasion, I said, "Hard to answer that one."

His eyes held mine. "Easier to list the bad ones?"

How true. I nodded.

"Me too." He looked up and smiled at the server who'd just arrived with the cakes and tea. As soon as she left, he leaned forward. I poured tea for us both. "The worst day of my life was the day I arrived at the hospital and saw Natalia after her attack. Until then I'd been able to hope that she wasn't as badly injured as they'd told me."

"Not when your parents died? I would've thought that would rate."

He gave a sharp laugh. "Not nearly. They were both so lost to me by then. By the time they were dead, I'd built my own life, one totally separate from theirs."

I closed my eyes, focused, and pulled up what I knew—what the whole world knew—about his mother and father: dissolute, pampered, royal jet-setters. Long divorced, each with a string of succeeding spouses. But they must have stayed friendly, because they died together, two drunks in a car crash.

I opened my eyes to see that he had a wry half-smile on his face. "What?" I said.

"You were just filing something away, right?"

Close enough. "I guess. Sometimes I'm not really aware I'm doing it."

He tapped his index finger noiselessly on the edge of the table. "If word got out about this . . . recess I'm taking and the things I've been saying—I mean, if it got out the wrong way, a lot of people would use that publicity as a reason to stop the peace negotiations."

"You're worried I'll open the file"—I tapped my head— "and sell the story of my night with a prince to some tabloid."

"Yes."

I leaned forward. "I would never do that, Tom. Not for a million dollars, not in a million years."

"I don't know why, but I believe you. Trust you." His smile broadened. "It should be a two-way thing, shouldn't it? So why not trust me and tell me about the worst day of your life. Or the best."

I picked up my fork and stabbed it into the cake. The food had been delicious, but suddenly everything seemed sour, probably because the guilt was roiling with all the talk about trust.

"Kelly?" he prompted softly.

I nodded. "The best day? This one might make the list. The worst?" I set down the fork. "As for the worst, well, let's just say, Tom, that my worst day was self-inflicted. And I'd like you to let me keep it buried in the past."

He looked like I'd jabbed the fork into him. "I'm sorry," he said. "It was rude of me. Pushy."

Pushy? I laughed, thinking of Kit. This guy didn't know pushy. "Tom Tomas Buckhorn Teronovich, you are the least pushy person I've ever met." I picked up my teacup and cradled it.

"It's just that we've spent the day together and I don't know who you are. Who are you, Delivery Girl?"

I'm a liar and a tease and an ex-junkie gofer who is trying her hardest to lead you into a trap, I thought. I haven't allowed myself to want something for a long time, and now it is my heart's desire to lead you into that trap.

He said, "Please?"

I have so little strength sometimes, so little defense against so many things. Guilt, for example, almost always wins. Over the last few hours I'd deceived him, hijacked him, laughed at him, forced him to give up an expensive suit. Maybe I owed him a crumb of truth. So I counted to three and I said, "I'm a recovering heroin addict, Tom. Nineteen years old and I've been clean going on two years. Obviously, I started young. I grew up in Dakota City and have never lived anywhere else. Grew up and messed up right here."

He searched carefully for the next thing to say, then hit wrong. "Your family—"

"No parents. I live with my aunt." Too close—I'd

brought it too close to what I needed to hide from him. "We're a bit alike that way, aren't we, Prince Tom?"

He nodded. "Did you quit playing violin because of the drugs?"

"Yes."

He reached out and took my hand. Held and looked at my fingers. It was a chaste, curious move. His thumb stroked mine. Okay, maybe it wasn't so chaste. "You told me earlier that you were very good. 'Once upon a time,' you said."

I pulled back. "I was very good. I started when I was three and by the time I was four, it was clear I was special, a prodigy."

"That's fun to picture. What sort of music does a four-year-old play?"

"Entry-level classical. But tougher stuff very soon."

"So you started using and had to give it up."

I shook my head. "No."

"You said—"

"I said I quit playing because of the dope. I quit playing *classical* for other reasons. I quit all that before I was using. It was a decision to quit. My decision."

"And why did you make that decision?"

I laid a hand over my teacup, letting the moist warmth push against my palm. There were a hundred and one answers, of course, and I'd heard them all in countless chem-dep counseling sessions. It was exhaustion. Fear of failing. Fear of success. Giving in to the desire to take charge of my life after years of never once being in charge.

"Kelly?" he prompted, his voice soft as fleece.

I met his gaze. "I fell in love with different music."

"What sort of different music?"

"We didn't know, that's just it; we felt like we were making it up. Jazz was a big part of it, and rock, certainly. Like I said, it felt like we were making it up. I didn't know what it was, the music I was discovering, but it was wonderful, and enticing enough to make me walk away from all the contests and competitions and the guest spots with orchestras." I saw his eyes dart away, and I reached for my water. "This is way more than you meant to hear. I'm sorry to go on so."

"No, keep going. I still don't see why playing violin is so dangerous for you."

I narrowed my eyes and sharpened my stare. "It's not like I can draw you a map, Tom. A life is not that simple."

"Neither are maps," he said. "So keep going, if you will."

"By the time I was fourteen, I was in a whole new world, meeting all sorts of musicians and artists and moving in their different circles. It was a huge change, because as much as I loved what I was doing and the music I was learning and making, I was no longer Kelly Ray, rising classical star. I'm not sure I knew who I was."

"So you tried to be like the people around you."

"Some of the people. Yes, you might say that having lost my own identity, I borrowed theirs."

"Hip heroin–using jazz musician."

Maybe it was simple after all. Like a straight line from one place to the next. I nodded. "By the time I was sixteen, I was using pretty heavily."

He leaned forward. "But surely something you love, something you do so well, surely that should be part of . . . getting healthy."

"Successful recovery depends on breaking old patterns."

He rolled his eyes and sat back. "Sounds like a therapist's line."

I leaned forward. The teacup tipped, and liquid sloshed and leeched through the paper tablecloth. "Ever been addicted to something, Prince Tom? Ever tried to quit and stay sober? It's hard. It's very hard."

"But to give up music? Can't you even play by yourself?"

"Playing with others, inventing something with other musicians, that was the thrill, Tom. And no audience, ever? What's the point of that?" I lifted my left hand, curved the fingers around a phantom violin neck. "I can still feel the strings, feel them vibrating. I hear the music, feel what it's like playing, making those sounds." I curled the fingers into a tight fist; my nails dug into the skin. "And when I do, I also feel the dope. I miss the music, Tom, but it was part of a life I can't live, maybe not ever again. So now I'm a delivery girl."

Someone's heart—his or mine—was pounding loud and fast. Boom, boom, boom.

He folded his hands on the table and studied them for a while. His eyes glanced up, looking past me, then they returned. "You said all of that as if you were saying it for the very first time."

Bingo, Tom, bingo. "I don't talk about it much."

His eyes again scanned the background. I definitely must have been boring him if outside was so much more interesting. He pulled his gaze back. "I'm sorry to ask this, but could you tell me what—"

Maybe it was his polite interest, or the weight of talking, but for some reason, I snapped. "No. I'm not going to tell you what it's like to use heroin. People always want to know, people always want the sordid details about using. What does it feel like? What made you do it? What were you thinking? It's like they want to get close to something that's out of bounds, something dangerous, but without the risk. And mostly I think they want to be entertained by my . . . mistakes."

I had his attention now. "You interrupted," he said tersely. "I wasn't asking about that." He leaned in. "Believe me, Kelly, I am not the least bit curious about the 'sordid details.' You know why? My parents were both drunks and my mother also loved her cocaine. They died together, and it was a lousy death. A pathetic drunk's death. I assure you: I'm not interested in being entertained by anyone's 'mistakes.'"

There it was again: boom, boom, boom. My heart, definitely mine. "I'm sorry, Tom. Sorry I jumped on you. Talking about it is just so hard."

"From the way you reacted, I'd say *not* talking is hard. Maybe you need more practice."

I inhaled deeply. Let it out slowly. "What question did I interrupt?"

He made a face. "Now I feel awful. This is so dumb—I mean, here you were, pouring it out, we're having this heart–to–heart thing when a day ago neither of us knew the other existed."

Speak for yourself, Prince Tomas Teronovich. "And . . . ?"

"So you're telling me all this, and I'm really listening and I'm glad that you're talking about it and I do want to know all about you, but meanwhile there's some sort of *thing* going on outside and I see all these people and I can't figure it out and you're talking about this serious stuff and I'm listening, I really am, but meanwhile, I can't help wondering: Why the hell are these ladies all dressed that way? Oh, that one is a guy; wow, nicely done. What's happening out there? Look."

I licked my lips, which had gone dry as I'd vented and raged, then pushed back my chair, turned, and looked. Outside, mixed in with the usual street scene, were several passersby clothed in period dress, dolled up for a party taking place in some other century. Hair piled high, hats, parasols, long slender dresses loaded with buttons.

"And now a lion?" he said in disbelief. I craned my neck. Coming toward us on the sidewalk was someone braving the heat in a full lion's costume. Behind him, two silvery men appeared. Tin men. They turned and entered the Midtown movie theater.

I laughed. "Oh, my gosh, I'd forgotten. I know what it's about. We did a show—" I stopped in time and held my tongue.

Luckily Tom was still staring and hadn't heard me. "What's going on?" he asked again.

"Do you really want to know?"

He faced me. "Please."

"It's Judy Garland's birthday."

two
that night

"Sing-along *Meet Me in St. Louis*? Sing-along *Wizard of Oz*? This is how you celebrate a dead actor's birthday? A little weird, isn't it?"

I handed Tom the popcorn and nudged him toward two empty seats. "This is nothing. This is just the party at the end of a film festival that kicked off a couple of weeks ago on her actual birthday. For real weirdness you'd have to go up north, to the town where she was born. There they have a huge blowout: a parade, carnival, Garland impersonators. They even used to fly in Munchkins."

"There's no such thing as Munchkins."

It was one of those moments when I seriously doubted his fitness to be king. Maybe the old men were right and he did need to be tucked away out of sight. I spoke slowly and clearly. "Of course, Tom, there is no such thing as a Munchkin. The actors, Tom, the actors. The ones who played the Munchkins. They bring in the actors."

He was not amused. "I still don't get it. A dead star's birthday? Why play dress-up?"

"She was born in Minnesota. We can't claim very

many celebrities, so we go nuts over the few we have. Whether or not they're all that big or even alive."

We'd settled into seats, clutching our popcorn and sodas. Two women in the row ahead of us turned. One laid down a scornful look. "Not that big? The greatest entertainer ever?" The woman next to her nodded. They both turned and faced front, simultaneously smoothing down the long skirts of their dresses.

I leaned forward and tapped the one who'd spoken. "Madame, would you kindly remove your hat?"

The Midtown is one of those great old theaters with fancy murals, red velvet seats, a balcony, and twinkling star lights. For tonight's event two huge monitors had been brought in and set up on either side of the screen.

By quarter of ten every seat was filled. There were plenty of people in costume: lots of long dresses of the style I guessed was from *Meet Me in St. Louis*, lots of Tin Men, dozens of Wicked Witches. By nine-fifty-five the clapping and stomping had started. When the lights went down, the monitors went on. People whistled and cheered.

Meet Me in St. Louis has a lot of catchy songs, but the sing-along was tentative at first. Of course, it was hard to watch the action on the screen, listen to the music, and manage to read the lyrics as they scrolled by on the monitors. But people got into other business: booing the stuffed-shirt dad; hissing the stuck-up school friend; ooh-ing and lip-smacking over the pretty boy-next-door.

And by the time Judy was riding the trolley with her crowd, headed to the 1903 World's Fair for a day of wholesome fun, the Dakota City theater was singing and rocking.

Prince Tom loved it. So did I.

When the lights went on and the music stopped, Tom leaned forward and tapped the lady on the shoulder. "That was wonderful," he said. "You were right."

The woman nodded. "'The Trolley Song' is simply the best movie musical number ever. Period."

A Tin Man sitting next to her companion turned around (stiffly). "Better than 'Over the Rainbow'? I don't think so."

I whispered to Tom. "It could get rough; want to leave?"

He looked at me as if I were nuts, then leaned forward to ask the Tin Man a question.

One of the *Meet Me in St. Louis* women in the row ahead crooked her finger. I leaned toward her. She whispered, "Your boyfriend is very sweet."

I glanced at Tom. He was reacting to something the Tin Man had said, rolling his eyes and laughing. I replied, "Yes, he is."

"Be good and be careful," she said as she turned back around.

One out of two, I figured. The best I could do for what remained of the night.

I checked my watch. *The Wizard of Oz* would start at midnight. I had ten minutes—should I call Kit? Would she be free to take the call? Was she alone? Was she even awake? I decided against calling. Either she was still being watched, or she was in bed. After all, on a normal night, she'd be sound asleep by now.

I looked around. Lions and tigers and bears, oh my; clearly, this was not a normal night. I wasn't alone in this conclusion: Just then people in the balcony unfurled and hung a banner that read "You're Not in Kansas Anymore."

Any reserve that had been shown during *Meet Me in St. Louis* was long gone by the time *Oz* began. It was no longer a movie; it was one raucous party.

But not when Garland sang the Rainbow song. Weirdly, for those few minutes, except for a few sniffles and sighs, the theater was dead silent. Then the song was over, wicked Almira Gulch came to call on Dorothy's family, and the party roared back to life.

I tugged on Tom's sleeve. "Anything like this in Lakveria?"

He shook his head, smiled, then pulled me closer and whispered in my ear, "When I am the king."

"I'm hungry."

"After all that popcorn?"

Tom wiped his hands on his jeans. "Buttered popcorn. What do you say, Kelly Ray?" He paused to savor the moronic rhyme. "What do you say we make a night of it? It's barely after two, and this may be my only chance ever to watch the sunrise in Dakota City. What have we got— three, four more hours until that happens?" He frowned.

"Of course, you probably have to go to work. What are you delivering tomorrow, any idea?"

You, Your Highness, you. "The good thing about my job, Tom, is that I never know what the day will bring. I'd be happy to pull an all-nighter with you, but I'd like to ask for one condition."

He was on some kind of high. The hour. The freedom. The movies and popcorn. "Ask me anything, Kelly Ray."

"After we watch the sunrise and before you go to the hotel, could you pop into my work and meet my boss? After I disappeared yesterday, I'm not sure how things are for me at the office. It would be great if I could introduce you."

"Would that help?"

"I'm sure it would. Promise?"

"I have a condition, too. Say yes to my condition and then I'll promise."

"What is it?"

"Would you buy me more food? When I went to the rest room between movies, some men there were talking about an all-night diner with great pie. Leo's. I heard raspberry is in season. No, wait, that's not right."

"Probably it is right. Leo makes great pie."

"No, I meant that it was two scarecrows talking about the pie. What do you say to this plan: raspberry pie at Leo's, a sunrise, your boss."

It should have been easy to agree. While I wasn't sure we wouldn't be intercepted by security at the station door, and I had no guarantee Tom would actually talk to

Kit, at least he was happy about staying with me. As long as I fed him.

But not Leo's. Anywhere but all-night Leo's.

Still, this was Dakota City. Where else could you go? The bars closed at one and so everything else shut down, too.

"You don't want to go there?" he asked.

"It's an old hangout," I said.

He understood right away and he gently touched my arm. "Old patterns, right? Well, some other place. It doesn't matter."

Old patterns. It was the closest either of us had come to referring to our after-dinner conversation. Four hours of Judy Garland and her costumed devotees had intervened, and now my prickly outburst seemed silly and distant. I slipped my arm through his and started walking. "There is no other place, not at this hour. If we were in the suburbs, we could go to a Perkins. But I'm not sure we're that desperate; besides, the buses quit running at two. There's another thing, though, about Leo's. The cops keep a close watch on the place. Leo doesn't allow stuff to go on inside, but . . ." I shrugged. "You can meet people there, make connections, or maybe hook up with a friend who might know where there's a party. So when they don't have real stuff going on, the cops come by and look tough."

"Then let's hope there's real stuff going on."

Luck held. The Dakota City police must have been busy with more serious things than looking for a runaway prince at an all-night diner. There were no patrol cars parked by the hydrant in front of Leo's.

No cops, but everything else was as I remembered: Leo was behind the counter, looking bored. Black plastic chairs and shiny stainless-steel tables. Ten red-topped stools at the counter. Black and white tile floor. Glittery jukebox programmed with sixty-three songs, all of them Etta James.

It had been two years since I'd been to Leo's. Two years since I sat on a stool and drank the coffee and ate the always-good pie. Two years. Not since that night.

That night I sat there, stool number three from the left, and chatted and flirted with Dewey Devine, falling (as always) under the spell of his rowdy red hair and icy blue eyes and red trumpeter's lips.

Whaddaya mean you can't come and play with us? Kelly, we need that violin. No one plays it like you. Baby-sitting, you've got to be kidding. How boring is that, come on now, Liz Turner's on bass. Okay, then, be good. Some other time, there might be some dates at the Jitter Joint, I'll keep you in mind, yeah, I mean it. Too bad you're too young for the real clubs. Baby-sitting. Oh, oh, oh, Kelly.

Then he whispered.

Here, hold out your hand, just so you know there's no hard feelings and that I'll love you forever. This, girl, is in case baby-sitting is as boring as it sounds, quick in the pocket, we don't want Leo to get mad. Tonight at eleven, exactly four hours from now, I'll do mine, you do yours, and no matter where we are, it will be like we're together.

If I remember it right (and who's to say that I do?), at that moment he kissed me here, touched me there. Exit Mr. Smooth.

Oh my God. And I *liked* him?

My laughter must have been louder than Etta's singing, because when I caught my breath I saw that everyone in Leo's was looking at me. "Sorry," I said.

"You okay?" Tom asked in the lowest of whispers.

"I'm fine. Just went off on a little memory riff. Habit of mine."

"Are you sure you want to stay? Are you really okay?"

"I am so fine, Mr. Buckhorn, I can't tell you. Maybe a little bit sad, but fine. Now let's get some pie."

We grabbed a table for two next to a large group of Tin Men and Dorothys. A waitress took our order and hustled away. She returned in a flash. Tom took one bite and set down his fork. "Oh, Kelly," he said.

"Yes?"

"I'm in love."

"The pie's that good?"

"It's that good. I'm in love with whoever made this pie."

I pointed to Leo, who was chewing a toothpick and working a crossword. Tom twisted and looked, turned back to his pie. "Maybe not," he said.

Not in love, but still hungry. He ordered seconds. While he was waiting, I went to the rest room. By the time I came out—it was a one-toilet bathroom and the two witches ahead of me were having trouble with their costumes—he was done with his pie, and three cops sat at the counter.

I slid into my seat. "What took so long?" he asked.

"The witches were having trouble with their skirts. See what's at the counter? Maybe we should go now."

He didn't look.

"Cops, Tom."

"I know. I saw them come in and I knew you'd be worried and then I realized I'd had enough, this was stupid."

"What are you saying?"

"I made a call. Leo's adding it to the bill; sorry. I didn't have change for the phone. I called my uncle while you were in the bathroom. Actually, I called his valet, Andre, on his cell phone. I thought that maybe at four in the morning it would be the best way to leave a message for my uncle; he is the king, after all. I'm just learning all this, but instinct tells me that you don't mess with an old king's sleep."

My mouth went dry and my heart slowed to a funeral beat. "What did he tell you?"

"What do you mean? I told Andre that I was fine, not to worry, I was out on the town, I was being discreet and no one would find out. I said that if they were still looking for me, they could stop because I'd be back. There's a breakfast meeting I'm supposed to attend, and I said that I'd be there. Why do you look like that? You should be pleased. You can relax, they won't bother us now."

Not on your life, I thought. Not as long as they think

you're with the ex–doper who works for the ruckus–raising one–armed radio host. "And then what did he say?" I asked slowly. Meaning, did he tell you who I was?

"Nothing. I hung up before he could say anything at all."

"Did you mention where we were?"

"Why does it matter now?" He tapped on the table. Obviously, the questions irked him. "It was the right thing to do. Maybe you should call home, too."

Home—there's a thought. "I can't."

His lips puckered a bit, but before he could say "Why?" I heard a familiar voice and knew immediately that it was all over. I was about to wake up from what must have been only a long, sweet dream. Stupid me. I'd been so worried about cops or bodyguards finding us. But I'd never once thought about running into someone who knew me. A loudmouthed, nosy someone.

"Well, look who's here!"

I turned in the chair. It wobbled a bit. "Hey, Sandi."

"Little late to be out on the town, isn't it?"

"Back atcha."

"Oh, but I'm not a working girl, I'm not the one who's always gotta run, gotta get to work." Sandi was a nosy loudmouth, for sure, but generally a good–hearted one. I'd only ever seen her at the St. Ambrose meetings, true, but there'd been six months of those, and I'd never seen or heard her so edgy. Sharp and edgy, ready to strike—you could almost feel it. I glanced at Tom. He was fixed on

Sandi, warily watching the woman as her fingertips riffled the sugar packs on our table.

I dropped my voice. "You okay? Drinking, maybe? Do you need to call someone?"

Birds have eyes like hers: dark, piercing, empty. "Drinking? You really think I'd be here if I'd started drinking again? Do you think I'd be standing here on my two feet if I were drinking or using again? If you ever listened, girl, you'd know my story. You'd know that when I crash, it's spectacular.

"And as for that phone call, I've already made one, and that's my problem, sweetheart. I called my daughter. It was her birthday. You know what's special about her birthday? Of course you don't, you don't listen. Her birthday is the one day of the year she allows me back into her life. Allows me a five-minute phone call. But of course it never lasts that long. She's like you, Kelly. Gotta run, gotta get to work, gotta go now. She's even sort of in the same business as you, she works for a newspaper in Chicago. She takes classified ads over the phone. Not nearly as glamorous as what you do, working for Kit Carpenter, world-famous radio host, but then we can't all have famous aunties, can we?" She took a breath, finally, and turned to give Tom the once-over. "You're cute. Want to join me at the counter? I'm old, sure, but I'm a much better listener than she is."

Sandi walked away, leaving Tom and me to stare at each other.

"Kit Carpenter is your aunt?" he said at last. The edge to his voice was razor-sharp; the chill in his voice was glacial. "I bet you're not really a delivery girl."

"I work for my aunt. I do her research and I run her errands. I guess that makes me Kit Carpenter's delivery girl. So, you know who my aunt is."

"Of course I do. Even if my uncle and the others hadn't been talking about her, I'd know."

"They were talking about her?"

"She was pestering everyone for interviews, they say. You know why that won't happen? Because they think she's uncontrollable. That's the word they used. Uncontrollable."

"Good for her. Why should all those old men think they can control her? Just because she goes after a story they don't want her to have, they call her uncontrollable?"

"Would you take a moment, Kelly, take just a moment to think about why they don't want her around? Can you possibly get it into your dope-soaked and detail-stuffed head why they don't want some rogue reporter tearing at them?"

I sat back. "Let's not get personal, Prince Tomas. Don't insult me."

He pushed on. "Something more than a story is at stake. My country."

I made a noise. "Your country, Tom Buckhorn? Tell me, when's the first time you ever set foot in Lakveria?"

He took a moment. "I'm not Texan," he said finally. "I'm not a British schoolboy. I'm Lakverian. My mother was

Lakverian, my father was, and all the people before them. My grandfather was king. His father was king. *His* father was king. I'll be the king. That's who I am. Look at how wrong it was for you to live with a borrowed identity, Kelly. Well, it's no different for me. I can't be anything but who I am. And I'm the crown prince of Lakveria."

He dropped his head in his hands. Rubbed his eyes. Looked up. "This whole day—it's just been one long lie, hasn't it? You led me along at the end of a lie, just to see what you could dig up. Get the guy talking, learn his secrets." He reached out and tapped my head, less gently than the time before. "And you filed it up there, tucked it away until you could turn it over to Kit Carpenter."

It took all the juice that I had, but I kept looking him straight in the eye, glare for glare. Steady on, Kelly. Keep it cool, keep it steady. Underneath the table, though, my foot tapped the real rhythm.

I pressed a hand on my knee. The tapping stopped. "Tom, I didn't set out to trick you into anything. When I ran into you at the hotel, it was just by chance. I really was simply taking a book to Simone."

"I believe that, but when you saw your chance, you ran with it. Smell of the chase and off you go. I don't know what you plan to do with your life, Kelly, but take it from me: You're a natural at your aunt's business."

"I'll take that as a compliment, Tom. And yes, I ran with it. Yes, I misled you."

"Misled?" He sat back. "You lied."

"Back at the hotel, when I was being mauled by your

thugs, what would you have done if I'd said, 'Why gosh, Your Highness, thank you for getting your two-legged Rottweilers off me. By the way, I work for Kit Carpenter, famous radio host. Howzabout coming on the show?' We both know that answer: You'd have cowered behind your bodyguards and whimpered until they put me on the elevator."

He fiddled with his fork and stared.

Let's not get personal, I had said. Don't insult me, I'd said. I flushed and looked down.

At the next table the Dorothys were rising to leave. I sat back and waited for the parade of blue gingham to pass. The last Dorothy paused, hesitated a moment, then plunged ahead: "We couldn't hear a thing, honest. But it sounded intense. You're both so darling; please make up." Then he patted my hand and joined the others.

Our waitress arrived with the check. She started to say something, but then read the mood, dropped the ticket and sped away.

I met his eyes again. "Please think about this, Tom," I said. "If I'd been straight from the start, you would never have met Simone, never heard her sing, and you'd have nothing to tell your sister. Nothing interesting, that is. Nothing special for her. Nothing that might make her squeeze your hand when you sit at her side."

He pointed a finger; it shook, he was that angry. "You are digging a deeper hole. When I told you about my sister, I was trusting you, I thought I was talking to a friend."

"Bull. You thought I was no one. You were under the

spell of Simone and you thought I was no one. Just an or-dinary girl to have fun with. You used me, too."

"Nice try, Kelly, but I'm not convinced. And if I did use you, it hardly compares, does it? I never lied about who I was and what I wanted."

"Oh yeah? 'Of course I want to lead my country.' You actually said that. And that's not a lie? Okay, sure, maybe you've reclaimed Lakveria as your homeland; we all have to be from somewhere. But I don't believe you want to be king."

He leaned back in the chair, folded his hands, closed his eyes. I waited.

"It's not a lie," he said.

"Then something's changed since we first met. If you're honest, you'll admit that."

"I think you give yourself too much credit."

A chunk of piecrust remained on my plate. I picked it up and crumbled it. I glanced up and saw that he'd pulled on the royal mask. The sweet eager guy—the one who'd gotten all teary over his sister, all hyper over the maps, and who'd belted out a melt-in-your-mouth bari-tone "We're off to see the Wizard"—was gone. Tom Buck-horn had definitely left the building.

Okay, my friend Tom was gone, but I still had Crown Prince Tomas Teronovich. And he was the one I'd wanted all along.

Right?

I took a slow breath. "I can help you, Prince Tomas. I can help you be king."

"I don't need your help. It will happen automatically when I turn twenty-one."

"When's that? Another year? Think your country will still be there?"

"Kelly."

"Talk to Kit. Let me introduce you to my aunt. Go on her show, and talk."

He pushed his chair back and started to rise. "Please just listen," I pleaded. "Hear me out. You know who she is, but do you know who her listeners are? There are millions of them. Mostly very conservative, exactly the people who normally mistrust the UN. Most of them are women. Go on her show and tell your story. They'll all be calling Congress within the hour demanding the payment of the UN pledge."

"What makes you think that will work?"

"I've heard your story. It will touch them. Talk about your sister."

"No."

"Kit will be on your side."

"Not from what I've heard."

"I know her better than anyone. She'll take one look at you and fall in love. And she'll listen to me and understand the story, the real story."

"Let me get this straight: You think I should go on the show, let your aunt the uncontrollable journalist babble about how cute I am, and then her millions of female listeners will fall into line?"

"They aren't malleable, I'm not saying that. They're smart, they think, they care. And when my aunt—the very serious journalist—gets them riled up about something, they make noise. And Kit will do it not because you're so damn cute, but because it's the right thing."

"I'm glad you think it's the right thing, Kelly. But I can't go meet with your aunt and I can't be on the show."

"Why not?"

"My uncle and your vice president and all the others might look to you like old men playing games and messing up, but they are trying. They truly are trying to get it right. I won't jeopardize their efforts. I will not risk it. I've already risked so much by spending the night with you."

He rose and left the table, then returned. He stood stiffly, arms at his sides, cool gaze fixed on me. "Thank you, Kelly, for most everything else. Thank you for feeding me and taking me to the library and to the movies and all of it, I can't even remember all of it. And yes, thank you for Simone." He slumped and briefly closed his eyes. When they opened, they were focused on something different. "And when I tell Natalia about the evening, I'll tell her about you." He again stood stiffly, and looked at me. "I'll tell her how, in spite of the lies, in spite of your . . . game, I'm grateful to you because for a few hours today I felt free again."

He was pushing open the diner door when I finally found my tongue, when my heart resumed beating. "You don't know the way back," I shouted. "Tom, wait!"

He waved me off with a sharp snap of his arm.

I fumbled my wallet as I pulled it out of my pocket. It bounced under the table and I dropped to my knees.

"He's getting away," someone said.

I pulled out some bills and threw them on the table.

"Go get him, girl," someone else said as I rushed past.

"Bye, baby, bye," Sandi said as I passed the counter. The cops, bless them, didn't speak or budge an inch.

Tom was headed the wrong way from downtown and his hotel. I ran and caught up, spun him around. "Do you want to know why I did it? Do you want to know why I led you around by a lie, as you so poetically put it?"

He planted his hands on his hips. "This is all getting way too dramatic. I'm exhausted and I want to sleep."

"Two years ago when I had that worst day of my life, she still didn't give up on me. So yes, I lied, and led you on, and used you, and had a hell of a lot of fun with you tonight, Prince Tomas. I wanted to give back something to my aunt Kit. I don't chase stories for the hunt. I went after this one for her. I wanted it for her."

He'd let his hands drop, and his shoulders had relaxed. But the eyes were still cold. "Don't expect me to weep over an addict's guilt or gratitude, Kelly. I won't play with the fate of a nation, with people's lives, just because you've managed to sober up and now you feel grateful."

I still had some bills in my hand. I held one out and said icily, "Here's ten bucks in case you see a cab. This time of night it's doubtful that you will, but you might get lucky. And downtown is that way. If you go left at the corner, you'll see a McDonald's. It's closed, but the cabs sometimes wait for calls in the parking lot."

He walked away without touching the money. After a few steps he halted, and without turning he said, "That woman in there, the one you brushed off? You really should go talk to her. She's on the edge, you can tell. Go talk to her, Kelly. Then you'll have done a good thing tonight, you can claim one very good thing."

"I'm sorry, Tom," I called as he walked away. "I'm sorry you think I'm that bad."

Sandi looked up from her coffee. "Lose the guy? That's too bad, sweetie."

I swung onto the stool. Third from the left, just like last time. "That was no guy, that was a prince."

She rocked her coffee cup. "You don't need to stay on my account, if that's why you're here. It's not as bad as it seems."

"I can stay."

"From the look of you, I'd say you're in no shape to support anyone. Barely holding yourself up, aren't you? Tough thing, to lose a guy."

"It's been a long day." Down at the far end of the counter the police rose to leave. I suppose I should have sent them after Tom, told them where to find the missing prince. Cruel, really, to leave him out on the streets.

Oh well. He was a big boy.

And, like Sandi said, I'd lost him. There'd be no interview for Kit, no applause for me. And to hear him moan, maybe I really had made things worse for the peacemakers. No way I could feel good about that.

Still, the look on his face when Simone laid down that kiss. And hearing her sing in the car. This excellent T-shirt. The goofy Garland fans.

And, okay, I'm not made of stone, so I had to admit to more that would leave a print: his sweet way with the funny professor. His mysterious scent. That incredible hair, those changeable eyes. The way that he listened to me.

Yes, I'd mucked it up good, but still, no regrets. With a little bit of time, no regrets.

Sandi signaled for a coffee refill, and the motion broke into my riff. I watched as she added two packs of sugar to the cup, stirred, and sipped. She rocked on the seat and hummed to herself. I could see dried blood around her nails, where she'd picked at her cuticles. Her mascara was smeared at the edge of her eye. Her lipstick was wide and uneven. Tom was right: She was teetering.

I said, "I understand if you don't want to talk to me, but there's got to be someone."

She snapped, "Don't bother yourself worrying. I'm here, aren't I, and not out trying to cop? That's a victory." She added a third sugar, stirred, and cradled the cup. A soft noise slipped out. A whispered wail, if there is such a thing. "I haven't had to call my sponsor in such a long time. Not since Tami's last birthday, anyway. One year. One year since the last call."

I swiveled my seat to face her. "Sandi, you're wrong

about something. I have too listened. Okay, you're right, I come to meetings and, sure, mostly I tune out, but I *have* heard you talk. And I've heard what you said, that you can't wait forever for someone to forgive you. None of us can wait for that because it probably won't ever happen."

She snorted. "I'd be happy to forgive myself."

"Wouldn't we all, but how likely is that?"

Sandi tossed back the rest of her coffee, rose, and marched over to the pay phone on the wall by the register. Leo looked up from his crossword.

I warmed the stool until she started talking, then made my exit, done with the night's one good thing. Sandi touched my shoulder as I passed.

Leo called out, "See you around."

What was that, I wondered: a good wish or bad?

Tom was perched on the fire hydrant outside, watching the diner door. I let it close behind me and stood there while I crossed my arms and hugged myself. "Change your mind about the cab fare?" I asked.

"I'll do it."

"Do what?"

"I'll go on the show. If you really think your aunt can make a difference, then I should do it." He wagged a pointing fist at me. "But I'm telling them first; it's only fair. I will not ambush their efforts."

Given the chance, they'd try to talk him out of it, maybe even restrain him and refuse to allow it to happen. Kit *was* uncontrollable; why would they risk letting him loose with her? "If you must, Tom. But if you go back to the hotel, they'll talk you out of it."

"Then I won't go back. I *will* call, though."

"Can it wait until morning, 'til we're at the station? That still gives your uncle time to tell the others. They won't be ambushed."

"Couldn't someone join me on the show, Kelly? I don't think I should do it alone. Could we compromise that way? Vice President Ripley, perhaps."

"I'm not sure that would work. He and Kit . . ." I paused, trying to be diplomatic. "Have issues."

"Someone, then? Don't you think it would be a good idea for Kit to have others than me to interview? More important people?"

The future king was pleading with me. Heady with power (or dopey from lack of sleep), I walked to him, rested my hand on his shoulder and said, "As you wish, Your Highness."

It took him a moment to decide if he was amused. He was; I felt him relax, saw the mask slip away. I stepped back.

"But only for the second hour, Tom. For the first half of the show, it's just you and Kit. Believe me, it will be stronger that way. You'll have a better chance of getting people on your side."

Maybe this prince did have a future in world politics: He saw the deal and knew it was a good one. Tom nodded. He checked his watch. Then he looked up at me, smiling for the first time since he'd been eating pie. "For a few more hours, then, I'm still all yours. What are we going to do now, Delivery Girl?"

Sleep would be nice. Once upon I time I would have thought nothing of making a bed on a park bench or in the shelter of a tree. But that was no way to host a prince, not if there were other options.

The trees on Kit's block were like sentinels, shadowy guards neatly spaced one to a house all the way down the street. "Which house is yours?" Tom said.

I pointed. "Second one in from the far corner, across the street. The corner one next to it, the one with the big porch? Vice President Ripley and his wife live there. Careful, don't step into the streetlight; stay close to this tree. I don't think we can go in."

He moaned. "Kelly, I am getting so tired of this hide-and-seek. Do you really think they might be watching your aunt's house at this hour?"

"See the corner room on the second floor, the one with all the lights on? That's my room, Tom. I never leave lights on and Kit never goes in there."

"So you're saying that's significant? Are you saying that your aunt turned your lights on as some sort of signal?"

"Lower your voice, okay? Sit down." I pulled him to the ground, and we leaned back against a tree trunk, blending into its silhouette. "It is a signal. She wanted me to think twice in case I came strolling home with you." I pointed. "I bet she was hoping I'd notice those two big black cars. I've never seen those cars parked on this street. Oh look, in the far one—someone just lit a cigarette."

He sighed. "What does it matter now? I promised you I'd be on your aunt's show. She gets the interview, Kelly. Don't you believe I have enough influence to make that happen? You think I'm that powerless? Why are you looking at me like that? What are you thinking, Kelly? You're holding back something you don't want to say; it's on your face."

I was so tired, I was beyond digging up the energy to keep lying. So tired from running and leading him along all night that I knew without a doubt I had used up all the lies forever. So I told him exactly what it was that had popped into my sleep-deprived brain. I said, "Has anyone ever called you Tommy?"

He won my heart forever: He didn't laugh. Just rested his head against the tree trunk and said, "Yes. One person. Isabel Fuentes. Lovely Isabel. Lovely brown-eyed, big-breasted Isabel."

Something about the way he said . . . the name. "Girlfriend?" I asked.

He was gone somewhere, a sweet memory ride. His eyes were closed and his thumb tapped a beat on his knee. "Even better than a girlfriend. Isabel was the world's best cook—my stepfather's cook, in Fort Worth. I can hear her now, hear her voice as she'd swat me on the head: 'Tommy, you little devil, get that brown Gypsy ass out of my kitchen before I make it black and blue.'"

This time he had to shush me. I was laughing. "Gypsy?" I asked.

"Of course. My great-grandmother was part Gypsy. You mean you don't have that fact filed away up there?" Okay, so he didn't really stroke my head, but it wasn't exactly a chaste tap, either.

I held still; so did he. The mysterious scent had been replaced by a warm male musk. That was nice, too.

His hand fell away. "We're part of it all, we Teronoviches. Muslim, Catholic, Lak, Mernot, Gypsy. We belong to everyone and—just by existing—we can offend everyone. The perfect choice for a not-quite-figurehead monarchy. Any wonder they voted to bring us back?"

"They brought back your family because your grandfather and great-uncle spent World War Two undermining Nazi control, and then when those bastards were gone, they held off the Soviets longer than any other Balkan nation."

"You do know the facts, Delivery Girl. Yes, all that happened. Before they were banished by the Soviets and settled down to fifty years of dissolute living. And now things are so bad that we're considered the last best hope for unity: the one Lakverian family with mixed blood. The mongrel royal family. Of course, no one's saying aloud the truth: that our blood is mixed blood because my forebears were wildly promiscuous."

"You won't be like that."

He settled in against the tree, drawing up his knees

and hugging them. "I won't. I want to be a good king. With all my heart, I want to help. And that's why, Kelly Ray, I think I should walk to one of those black cars, turn myself in, and go back to the hotel. I'll round up every world leader I can find and bring them to your uncontrollable aunt Kit. I'll make them do it. I know now I can do that if I want to. It's my country we're talking about, isn't it?"

I should have leaped into his arms, right?

"What do you say?" Tom continued. "Shall I round up the politicians and we give Aunt Kit her dream interview? Isn't that what you wanted?"

"I'm worried."

"I promise: It will happen."

"I'm worried about Kit."

"Why? From all I've heard, she can more than handle that sort of thing."

"She can, and that's what worries me. Tom, I know exactly what she'll do with a set-up like that: Play those guys, and you, like you're puppets. Look, she's all I've got in the world. My family, that's Kit. But I know her. She'll see her chance and she'll go for blood. She'll have the time of her life and that won't help a thing. It could even jeopardize what you're trying to get done." I licked my lips. "Believe it or not, I care about that now."

"So they were right about her?"

"Yes. They were so very right." I looked up and smiled, though I don't know if he could see that in the half light.

"So why should *I* go near her?"

"Because it's not the same story and she'll see the difference. You telling your story, your hopes—that's a world apart from an interview with the old wise men clearing their throats and being careful about what they say. Be Prince Charming, Tom, and get her on your side. Then she'll want to get her listeners on your side, and once that happens—once she figures out what they need to hear to understand—you'll have it. Most of her millions of listeners will head to the phones to tell Congress to pay that UN bill, and you will have what you want."

"I don't know," he whispered.

For twelve hours I'd been one-on-one with this guy and I had been so good. (If you don't count the lying.) I mean, he was the best-looking guy I'd ever been this close to, and I had been so good about not touching him.

But I touched him now. Reached out to the side of his head and, imitating the very bad accent he had used, said, "Tommy, you leetle Geepsee devil; do it my way."

Hey, it had worked for Isabel, right? Of course, I didn't swat him the way he said she always did. Maybe I meant to when I first reached out, but I just couldn't. I mean, swat a prince? Instead, I ran my hands through that hair, that luscious, wavy dark hair.

Before I could pull my hand back, his head sort of dropped against my open hand. I held still. He closed his eyes.

I looked at the line of his jaw and the curve of his

neck, and felt the warmth and the weight on my palm. It would have been so easy just to lean a bit forward and pull him a bit closer . . .

I'll never be sure, but I think I heard him whisper (the softest of whispers), "I can't."

And I think I whispered back, "I know."

I pulled my arm away. His eyes flickered open and stared into the dark. And finally he said, "We'll do it your way, Kelly."

"Thank you, Tom."

He dropped his head to rest against the tree. "But what do we do until then? Go to the station? Or does your instinct for cloak-and-dagger tell you that my uncle's men are watching for me there, too?"

I checked my watch. "Could be. Probably." And my temporary ID didn't allow me access until morning.

"So they're going to get me any way we do it. Back to square one: I go to the guys in the big dark cars."

"No. I promise that I'll get you in the station, and once you're in Kit's office, they can't touch you until we want them to."

"And how are you going to get me past the international security you imagine is in place? Do you have a plan for that?"

Not yet, but why tell him? "Trust me, okay?"

I had to shush him again, he laughed so hard at that. "'Trust me,'" he mimicked. "As if I haven't been, and look where it's got me. Okay, Kelly, I'll trust you; now back to my question. It's almost four. What now? Do you at least have a plan for now?"

"I do have a plan," I said. "That is, if you still want to see the sunrise."

From Kit's place it's a ten-minute walk through neighborhood side streets and along the lake drive to the canoe racks on the north shore of Lake Lucille. I didn't tell Prince Tom what I had in mind, because I gave it even odds that once he knew my plan involved more physical exertion, he'd drop to his feet and refuse to budge.

The houses bordering the lake were Dakota City's showplaces, some of them worthy of even a prince's wonder. "That one?" I pointed as we strolled. "When it was built in 1909, it was the most expensive house west of Chicago and it sat vacant for seven years before anyone ever moved in, because of a divorce dispute. They had them back then, too. The white one coming up? It had the first electric lights in Dakota City. And the house two doors over from it—you can't see it too well because of the trees—three murders in sixty years, right in that house. Who'd want to live there anymore, don't you wonder?"

Tom paused and looked at me, eyes wide in amazement. "Do you ever feel like you're going to explode from being stuffed with so much trivia?"

"I do sometimes. But I can't help myself, I keep soaking it up."

"You must not have had a horribly bad habit, Kelly, if your brain is that nimble."

"Bad enough. The one on the corner? Frank Lloyd Wright. There are three of his on the lake, but we won't be walking by the others."

"Why not?"

"Because we stop here. Turn, watch your step. Now be a good boy, sit on this bench for a while, and watch for cop cars while I get the canoe down. I doubt if we'll get caught, I never have, but still; I'm about to turn you into a criminal, Tom."

"You've got to be kidding, we're not—"

"Hush, don't say a thing. Voices carry across the water, and who knows—someone else might be up. And yes, we are."

There were forty-five canoes stored on the racks. Fifteen stands, three high. My Old Town was on the top bar of an end column. I twirled the numbers on the combination, heard the click, pulled it open. The paddles and life vest I'd secured under a seat shifted free as I pulled the lock and cable. I yanked the life vest out and tossed it to Tom.

"I can swim," he said.

"I told you to be quiet. And I don't care if you can; I'm not going to risk a royal drowning."

"What about you?"

I can swim better, I would have answered, but didn't for two reasons: One, voices really did carry over water, and two, headlights were zooming along Lake Drive toward us. "Lie down on the bench and be still," I said just before stepping into the shadows between rows of canoes.

The car passed. As soon as the brake lights were out of sight, I went back to work. I checked that the paddles were still wedged securely under the thwarts, then slid the canoe off the rack, easing it over my head and settling the portage pads onto my shoulders. I backed up slowly until I could turn and head down toward the dock.

Tom whispered "Wow" as I passed the bench. Down on the dock I crouched, jutted a knee, rolled the canoe off my shoulders, and rested it on the knee a moment before lowering it onto the water. Tom joined me, kneeling beside me as I caught my breath. I sat on the dock and kept the canoe in place with my foot. "Wow," he said again.

"Hold the applause until we're on the water," I said.

"Should I ask whose canoe we're taking?"

"Mine."

"Then why is this a criminal act?"

He had put on the vest but it wasn't zipped. I loosened the side straps so it would fit and zipped him in. "Technically speaking, the lake is a city park. And technically, parks are closed from sunset until sunrise. I've only ever heard of the police tagging people coming or going. Once we're out on the water we're okay, and it will be light by the time we come back." I held out a paddle. "Let's go."

I could tell immediately by the way he handled it that he would be less than useless. I took it back. "Never mind. Get in, sit still, and I'll paddle. Let's move. No, don't sit on the seat, on the bottom."

He started to whine, but I growled. "You're less of a hazard sitting low; besides, you can lean back against the thwart and rest. That bar is a thwart. Get in."

The future king obeyed my command. In seconds we were moving, my long strokes sending us skimming across the still, dark water.

There are five lakes in Dakota City. Lake Lucille is the smallest—too small for sailing, but ideal for kayaking and canoeing because of its several bays and three islands. Motorized craft are prohibited on all the city lakes. Of course, what Tom and I were doing was also prohibited and, well, here we were. But thankfully, people observed the motor ban.

We weren't the only ones out. A kayak emerged from an island cove. The kayaker and I raised paddles, criminal saluting criminal.

Our canoe glided on. "See that brick house, the one with the light on the third floor?" I whispered to Tom, pointing with my paddle.

"Mmmm," he said, nestling down, getting comfortable.

"Every time I'm out here, that light is on, no matter how late at night, no matter how early in the morning. Twice I've seen a woman dancing in the room—dancing alone."

There was more and I showed him all of it. The house with neon blue lightning bolts flashing in the second-story windows. The house with ten chimneys. And of course, my candidate for weirdest.

"Mannequins? A living room full of mannequins?" Tom's voice cracked in wonder. "And don't they ever get complaints about those orange lights? Are they on all the time? People must complain."

"They're not just mannequins, it's an art installation. The lights are on all the time. I've heard that the only people who've complained are some neighborhood bird-ers who say the constant light might disturb nesting patterns for a family of linnets supposedly living in a tree somewhere along here." I paddled on.

"Do you come out here often?"

Only on the bad nights, I started to say. Then I realized that, at least tonight, that wasn't true. "Pretty often," I said.

"Ever come during the day, like normal people?"

"What's the fun in that? You can't see into houses."

He shifted and the canoe rocked. "Steady," I said. "I don't want to go in the water. It's not very deep, and the bottom's weedy and mucky."

"So you get your kicks from watching people's houses. Kinky." He reached out and dragged a hand in the water.

I pulled in my paddle. We drifted, with only the breeze pushing us along. "I'm not interested in all the houses." I pointed my paddle; water trickled off the blade. "Mostly that one."

He looked. "Nice, but compared to the others it's pretty ordinary."

"We can't all live in palaces, Prince Tom. And it's not ordinary at all. That was my house; I grew up there. Well,

I lived there until I was twelve, until my mother fell in love for the second time and got married for the first time. It belonged to my grandparents, my father's parents."

Now he was interested. "You mean your mother—who wasn't married to your father—lived with his parents until she fell in love with someone who wasn't their son? That sounds as twisted as European royalty. No wonder we get along, Kelly."

"They were happy to have us. I was their only grandchild and they wanted me reared properly. That is, what *they* considered proper. So they opened their doors and sucked us in. No one ever came right out and told me, but I'm pretty sure that they let my mother know they would fight her for me. Live with them—live like them—or lose me. And when it was clear so early on that I could do something special with the violin, well, that sealed the deal. My music was expensive—the lessons, the instruments, the travel. My mother could never have afforded to pay for it. So they . . . bought us."

"That's harsh, Kelly."

"But that's how it was. They gave us shelter and paid for my music, and in return they took control. Well, mostly it was her; my grandfather died when I was five."

"Your grandmother took control of your training?"

"Control of our lives. She meant well, I know, but with every single thing she gave, there were strings attached. That's a dangerous way to live and love, Tom. After a while those strings get twisted and people get caught up and maybe even strangled."

"But she was trying to help. You can't blame her for you being a drug addict."

"I don't," I snapped. "I didn't say that, and I don't want you to think for a moment that I'm into passing off blame. I did what I did, Tom; I made the choice. I'm the one who jumped into the deep dark hole and I'm the one climbing out."

"If your grandmother was so into control, how did she feel when your mother fell in love with someone who wasn't her son?"

"Oh, she was happy about that. He was someone she liked, a son of a friend. Billy. Imagine: a grown man named Billy."

"And where was your dad? What say did he have in all of this?"

"None whatsoever. No one had seen him in years. I've never seen him at all, not once in my life." I let him take time to digest it, gave him all the time in the world.

Tom stared at the house without speaking. "So the delivery girl grew up in the swankiest neighborhood," he finally said. "Does that make you Dakota City royalty?"

"Hardly. My grandfather was just a plain old hardworking lawyer, and she was a tireless volunteer with all the right charities. They climbed up the ladder by working, climbed up to a nice big house on Lake Lucille."

"When did your mother die?"

"She didn't." I tipped my head. "She lives there, right there in my grandparents' house. With Billy and . . . their little girl. Not with my grandmother of course. She died last spring."

"But you said your parents were dead. Another lie?"

"I didn't say they were dead, Tom. I didn't lie about that. I said that I had no family except for my aunt, and that's true. My father has been gone forever, and for some time now she's been gone from my life." I picked up the paddle and stroked twice, straightening the canoe, keeping it pointed toward shore. "I think the little girl's room is the one on the left, second floor. See the glow—a night-light, don't you suppose?"

"The 'little girl' is your sister, your half sister?"

"Her name is Louisa. She's going on three."

"And is she gone from your life, too?"

"That's right. That's how it is." I resumed paddling, turning the craft away from shore and heading it toward the widest part of the lake. "Daylight pretty soon, we need to get out of this bay if you want a view of the sunrise." Or if we didn't want to be spotted watching the house.

The sky was lightening. A few cars were turning onto the lake drive. A lone runner moved along the pedestrian path. Morning.

Tom twisted until he could see me. He said, "What's the story, Kelly? What happened?"

A kayak whizzed out at racing speed from between the islands, passed us, and was gone, headed toward the lagoon leading to another lake. I pointed. "If we go that way, we connect with all the lakes. We could spend the day on the water, going from lake to lake."

He waited.

"Please understand, Tom, that I don't feel sorry for myself. There's no self-pity. I just look at the facts and say I did what I did and that's how it is. I hurt them very badly. I was dangerous to them and they did what they did to protect themselves from being hurt again. And that's what anyone should do. Isn't that what you did? Built a life separate from your parents' to keep yourself safe? Yes, it's the right thing to do."

He said, "Tell me the story."

Drug stories are boring, Tom, they're even worse than family stories, so don't worry, I won't bore you much with all that. Won't bother you with the story of fights with my mom—after all, who doesn't fight with her mom? But you know, I don't like to use the word. *Mom.* I don't have a claim on that word, not anymore.

Really, the fights weren't even that bad. Typical stuff. Not bad at all, not even when I quit the violin grind. Guess what she said about that. "If that's how you feel, then it's fine. Go find something else, but whatever it is, be good at what you do." And I remember thinking, What sort of reaction is that? All those years, all the work, and that's all she can say? "Be good at what you do"? I mean, didn't she care? But that's what she said when I pulled the plug on everyone's dream.

Which was considerably different from my grandmother's reaction. There was nothing in-different about that. As soon as she heard, she raced to where I was, and the first thing she did was put her hands on my shoulders—God, I can still feel those hands on my shoulders—and she said, "After all I've done for you..." And then she couldn't go on, she was so livid.

It wasn't the last time I heard her say that very same thing. I gave her plenty of oppor-tunities to say it again.

You know how I did it, how I walked away from it all? I was playing—in the middle of ac-tually playing for judges in a big competition, my third that year. It was Chicago, the Mid-west Musicians of the Future, a very big deal, at least in that world. I'd come in second place the year before, and this year was supposed to be mine. I think it could've been, except for one thing. I didn't want it.

But there I was and I was trying. Playing a Paganini sonata. I was nailing it, too. Well, if I look at it clearly, maybe I wasn't nailing it, be-cause I wasn't focused. And then there I was in the third bar of the second movement, and suddenly I was thinking, Screw this. I don't want to do this anymore. And so I sailed out of Paganini into an Andrew Bird motif. And I finished and said to the judges, "Wasn't that a whole lot nicer?" Then I packed up and left. And later when everyone asked, Why? I said, I'm done. I'm done with this forever.

But I wasn't done, not with the music, just with that music. I started playing other stuff, with other musicians. I was learning a whole new sound and living a whole new life. As much as you can when you're barely fifteen. But it was enough, and I got in over my head.

It wasn't like I had a gutter-sniffing habit. I never progressed to needles. I always had access to money, so I never had to steal or do worse to get stuff. A very middle-class habit, Tom. But a habit just the same and you can't hide it forever. When they found out I was using, they packed me up and shipped me off to rehab. One month to a new life.

I was lucky, I guess, to have people who cared, who took action. My grandmother visited whenever they let her, which was often enough. And why not? She was paying. She'd come for an hour and we would have tea. And when the hour was over, she'd kiss me once on each cheek and say the very same thing she said before every recital, every concert, every competition.

Don't disappoint me.

That's when Kit enters the story. She heard what was happening and knew what it meant. Knew how my grandmother—her mother—would be trying to deal with things, control the situation, take charge. Kit quit her job and moved here, just to be close. Gave up the writing and reporting and started talking about movies and menopause with America so she'd have something to do while she set-tled down in Dakota City. She did all that to be an option for me. An option to my grand-mother's iron will. She knew about that iron will, of course. She was her mother's oldest child and she knew.

When I got out of rehab, I moved in with Kit. Everyone agreed that it might be better. Everyone agreed we had to try something new. I'll say this: I didn't start again right away. I didn't want to start again at all, but it was there by then; it was in me. The longing was in me.

Up to a point it's easy enough to hide that you're using. So when I did start again, no one knew. I was careful this time not to be gone at night and raise questions. Careful to keep the pattern of using under control. Up to a point you can do that. I was careful to wait until Kit was asleep or gone. Poor Kit. She never knew, never saw what was happening. No one did, of course, but I was living under her roof. Her mother never forgave her for that.

About the time I started using again, they had a baby, Billy and my moth—oh, let's call her by name. Her name is Ann. They wanted to make a show of trust, of confidence in me. They let me baby-sit from time to time.

She was a beautiful baby, Tom. I could always stop her crying. I could always get her to laugh. She loved me. Took a bottle from me and only me. When it came to eating, she wanted to be nursed by her mother or she wanted me. Five months old. That's how old she was the last time I saw her.

Up 'til then, I swear, I never did anything when I was with her, especially not when I was taking care of her. And I don't know why I did that time, except I started feeling sorry for myself. That's why I don't get into feeling sorry for myself, Tom, because then it's easy to do stupid things, and stupid things can be dangerous.

But that night I did. I broke my rule. First, though, I took care of her. Fed her, walked her, sang to her, held her, changed her. It was a very hot night, a lot like tonight was. So I had her in just diapers and a T-shirt. A little pink T-shirt. I put her in bed, pulled the shirt down over her belly, and turned out the light.

Then I went to the room that used to be mine and I turned on the radio. Am I boring you? All these details? I think I'm just now remembering these details; forgive me.

I turned on the radio, mistake number one. I lit candles, mistake number two. The radio was tuned to 88.5, "Jazz Overnight," live that night from Club Chase. I tuned in to other people playing while I was watching a baby, and whaddaya know, I started feeling sorry for myself, lying there in my old room with its pastels and lace curtains and sweet little flowers on everything.

Then I must have reached in my pocket. Mistake number three, because that's when I found the dope a friend had given me earlier that evening. At Leo's—I'd picked it up at Leo's.

I remember that the radio announcer talked between sets about the meteor shower going on outside, and I must have thought, Hey, go outside and see. So I did. Mistake number—oh, what does it matter. I went outside, and the sky was ablaze with falling stars, all right. Billy and Ann didn't live in the lake house then, it was another. They moved in here when my grandmother died last year.

They weren't her kids, but she liked them better than she had ever liked her own. So she left them her money, her house, her charity work, her place in the life of this city.

Back then, though, they lived in their own house. Smaller, but with a huge yard rimmed with lilacs. I can't remember if they were in bloom. And I lay in the backyard and watched the sky. No: First I snorted my bag, then I lay back and watched the sky.

A heroin high isn't the same every time. Sometimes I'd start with a pure manic single-minded rush, where I'd get this goal in my head and that's all I could think about, do, see. I used to clean a lot, those times. Middle of the night I'd be cleaning my room or scrubbing my bathroom. Reorganizing the books in Kit's library—I did that more than once. She's a sound sleeper, my aunt.

But sometimes it takes you the other way. Most times, maybe. A lockdown, that's how I think of it. There's no noise, no thought, no feeling. There's no one watching or talking or judging. It's all just shut out. Everything shuts down. That's how it was that night when I went out to look at the stars. In the whole wide world, it was just me and the stars, one after another, falling out of the sky.

You can finish the story, right? You can figure what happened next, *how* it happened? The candles, the curtains. The baby–sitter, useless, nodding off in the backyard. That's where they found me, wasted, untouched by the fire, not even aroused by the fire. While the baby . . .

She didn't die. They got to her through that smoke and heat. One lung was destroyed, but she didn't die. You might say, Tom, that it was the one good thing about that night.

No, there's a second. The moment they heard that the firemen had found me—how they had found me—in the yard, Billy and Ann put up a wall. Built a big solid wall between my life and theirs. And I'm glad they did it. I mean it, believe me; with all of my heart I'm glad they did it.

I'll never hurt her again.

I picked up the paddle and straightened us out, pointed us east. I was hoping hard that Tom would stay quiet. I didn't want to hear what he was thinking, not now. Didn't want to deal with judgment of any type, didn't want—

"Tom! What are you doing? Don't stand up in a canoe!" But he didn't heed me and he rose to his feet. The paddle nearly flipped out of my hand when I grabbed the gunwales, trying to steady the rocking. The paddle dropped to the canoe floor with a loud clang that echoed across the water.

"You're going to tip us. Tom! You can't just stand up and turn around in a canoe."

"I want to look at you."

"Well, look at me later. Besides, the sun's coming up over there. Now you're sitting the wrong way."

"I'm not going to tip us. Quit your moaning. Oh, Kelly, you shouldn't have made me give up the suit at the thrift shop. I had a handkerchief in it. You could use one." He settled in. "All safe."

I rolled my eyes. Wiped my face with the back of my hand.

"We're a lot alike," he said.

"I don't see the least bit of similarity. For one thing, I know how to behave in a canoe."

He smiled. "As I was saying: a lot alike. Our families are a mess. And we both have sisters just out of reach."

I rolled the paddle in my hand, the smooth wood a familiar comfort. "Even if there is a resemblance, Prince Tom, that's where it ends, because mine is better off for the separation."

Tom raked me over with those changeable eyes. Then after a very long time he said, "Is your mother beautiful, too?"

I looked at the house one more time before setting my paddle in and steering us away. I nodded and whispered, "Very beautiful. Athletic. She had a wonderful laugh. She painted and sewed. She made such gorgeous things. Quilts, you should see the quilts she made."

"You make it sound like she's dead. Tell me more. Tell me another nice thing about her."

I thought for a moment. "*She* never once said 'Don't disappoint me.' I never once heard it from her. Just that one weird thing: 'Be good at what you do.' But you know, now that I think about it again, I can see that maybe it's kind of a wish, isn't it? A wish for someone you . . ."

"Someone you love?"

I didn't answer.

He flicked his hand in the water, scattering drops. "So when you did disappoint her, it really mattered."

"I've said enough, Tom."

"Tell me about—"

"Nothing more. You've pushed me this far, Your Highness. Any more, and I'll push you—into the water. The sun's coming up. You'd better look; after all, that's why we're here."

My eyes were on the distant lakeshore, but I could feel him looking at me, deciding how far he could go.

He was no moron. "All right then," he said cheerfully. "Let's watch the darn sun. I guess I'd better change position." He stood up, waited until he had my attention, then grinned and rocked the canoe. Ha ha, it's a joke, his dopey look said, but then that vanished when the canoe kept on rocking with a rhythm of its own. He tilted on one foot, arms flailing, weight shifting. I set down the paddle, dropped low to my knees, grabbed the gunwales to steady things, and ordered him to sit.

He obeyed the command, shifting around slowly so he was facing front. He sat down low, leaned back against the thwart, and relaxed. I was still on my knees, and his hair brushed my cheek as he settled.

"Pretty sunrise," he said.

"See that silver streak between the trees?"

"No."

I pointed. "Between the spiky pine and that big round oak. That's the university art museum. It's at least three miles away, but it's on the town's only hill and we can see it way over here. It has stainless-steel walls and they reflect the light like you wouldn't believe. There, that flash, did you see it?"

Tom didn't say. He simply pulled my arm down, set it across his chest and held it in place. Then (what the hell) I wrapped the other one around him and rested my chin on his head.

Oh, a canoe is a dangerous place. Not because you're one stupid move from cold weedy water. But because there you are, just the two of you, with maybe all the time in the world to talk. Or not talk, and that's dangerous, too.

After a while, a nice long while, he spoke. "When I go back to Lakveria," he said softly, "it's likely I'll be killed. The terrorists won't give up 'til they've done that. They thrive with chaos. They get rich from the chaos. Any hint of order or peace is a threat. That's what Natalia was, a threat. She was becoming respected, maybe loved, and that suggested the possibility of peace. Anything that could remotely unify the Lakverians, they'll want to destroy. I'm a target, Kelly Ray."

"You have security."

His chest moved under my hands as he laughed. "It was no match for you and Simone."

"Don't go back to Lakveria. Don't let them make you king."

"I have to. It's who I am, and it's what I have to do. There's a chance I might help, Kelly, there's a chance things can be better. If I can help that to happen, then Natalia's suffering won't be for nothing. That makes it all worth it to me. It's as simple as that.

"It's what I have to do," he repeated softly. "I will, and I want to, but sometimes I feel like I just don't know how."

"One day at a time, Prince Tom. Take it one day at a time."

He crisscrossed my hands under his, squeezed them tight, and then said, "Look!" just as the sun broke over the trees, opening up another fine summer day.

three

---

talk now

There were three police cars in the small lot near the canoe racks. Tom shrugged and said "Hardly matters now" when I pointed them out, but I wasn't so blasé. It didn't matter what had been said and what promises he'd made; I wouldn't rest until I'd made the delivery.

The officers were rousting figures sprawled near a cluster of trees on the boulevard. Bottle necks protruded from three brown paper bags. The rousting wasn't work enough for six men and women, so one of the officers sauntered over to the racks as I was securing the canoe.

"Gonna be a hot one," he said. "Six a.m. and already seventy-eight degrees. I bet it was nice and cool out on the water."

"Nice as can be," said Tom.

I glanced over to the other cops. They had successfully hauled the men up and were guiding them to separate patrol cars, offering a one-way ticket to detox. Yet another of the cops walked toward us. "Whatcha got, partner?" he asked the one with us.

"Just a couple of lovebirds back from a morning paddle."

I could feel the heat of his partner's gaze on my back as I locked up the canoe. I emerged from the racks and grabbed Tom's hand. "Let's go," I said.

"I've been waiting for you," he answered. Then he flashed a royal smile on the two policemen and said, "We both have to get to work."

Cop number two looked us over, up and down. "Work?" he snorted. "Dressed like that?" His thumb tapped on his wide gun–bearing belt.

"Hey, Dan, let it go," said cop number one. Dan didn't budge, just studied Tom and me.

I spotted a bus coming down Franklin Hill. "Have a great day, officers," I said with false cheer. I kept hold of Tom's hand as I led him away, trying not to look like I was fleeing.

Tom whispered to me, "We could have gotten a ride, I bet."

"We have a ride. Hurry up, Your Highness, your coach has arrived."

I glanced back once we were seated on the bus. The two men had returned to their car. Officer Dan stood watching the bus pull away.

Dakota City buses converge downtown at Water and Ninth. At this hour it was mostly worker bees coming and going, and Tom and I blended into the cheerless throng as we stepped off the bus. I half expected to be met by a blockade of patrol cars and a line of cops, led by suspicious Officer Dan, but as I scanned the crowds, the only official person in sight was a city transit worker, peering into the wiring of a dead traffic signal.

The parking ramp attendant was in her booth when I led Tom from the sidewalk onto the ramp. She pointed energetically toward the pedestrian walkway. I blew her a kiss. "She hates it when you don't stay on the sidewalk," a voice behind me said. I turned and saw Miller, the KLIP security guard, headed in to work. "Once she even ran out of her booth and yelled that I was jeopardizing her job and my life by taking the shortcut."

A souped-up Beetle roared past. "Perhaps she has a point," Tom said after he'd jumped to safety.

Miller looked him over, making a very close study. Then he turned to me and said, "Good morning to you, Kelly. I have to say, thanks to your aunt and yourself, that yesterday turned out to be one of the more interesting workdays I've had here at KLIP." A BMW roared onto the ramp, and Miller and I joined Tom on the sidewalk. Miller motioned toward Tom. "Is this the young man with whom you were on the lam?"

"Yes. What happened?"

"What happened and what I heard was happening from the talk in the cafeteria, being not entirely the same thing, together make up an interesting story." He faced Tom and bowed. "Your Highness." He straightened. "Though I must say, dressed as you are, I would never have guessed. And what sort of accent do I detect?"

"Texas," I said impatiently. "What's the story?"

"Around four o'clock, just as I was taking a break to get refreshed for the double shift I agreed to work since Tony Herbert called in sick, though I suspect that wasn't precisely the situation considering the Red Sox are in town for three and Tony, who was to have relieved me, is a very homesick native of Boston—"

"Miller, please. What happened?"

He shrugged. "The place was crawling with cops and bodyguards. One was even assigned to keep me company, which wasn't too bad a thing because he played a nice game of gin. About nine o'clock, though, most of them were pulled off, but the orders were still clear: If you returned to the station, they were to be notified at once. And if you were accompanied by anyone, you were both to be personally escorted to the security office, where you would be courteously detained. Under no circumstances was your companion to be allowed upstairs to Ms. Carpenter's office." He checked his watch. "Talk about being detained. I was hoping to grab a bite in the cafeteria before I punched in."

"So that's what happened; what was it you heard?" Tom asked, walking along with Miller.

"That Kelly was painting the town with a prince. No one was sure, though, if she was taking orders from her aunt to rope in an interview, or"—he shrugged again—"showing you a good time and partying. Maybe the way she used to. Which would sadden us all."

"We did have a good time," Tom said, "while she roped me in for an interview. And no one needs to be sad."

Maybe getting inside wasn't going to be as easy as walking in and saying hi to whoever was on duty. "Think they'll stop us from going in?"

Miller's eyes widened. "I don't know what 'they'll' do, but if yesterday's instructions are still operational, I'll stop you."

"Miller, please."

"No way, Kelly. You're a nice girl with a friendly word for me every time you come to work, but I won't do it. I'm not risking my job, not a chance."

We'd moved off the sidewalk and were standing in an empty spot with a Reserved sign painted on the concrete column. A Lexus honked and flashed its lights as it angled in, bullying us out of the space.

"The jig is up," Miller said. "I'm turning you in."

"Miller, if you—"

He smiled and held up a hand. "I'll tell you what I always told my two girls: Don't whine and don't beg. Give me reasons to do something, and if they're good ones, well, then I'm reasonable. But, Kelly, not this. Why, you don't even have your ID on. Ignoring that alone could get me fired." Miller resumed the walk to the station entrance.

"I've got my ID," I said, and grabbed my wallet. As I removed the plastic card, I saw something else.

I pulled out the answer to everything. "Miller, stop," I said. "How about a deal?"

He waved to the guard standing in the booth at the entrance of the radio station. The man waved back.

"You've held me up long enough," Miller said to me, "and now Petey won't want to wait while I get my bagel."

"Just a minute more," I said. "And don't worry about something to eat because I'll send down something from Kit's office. She gets muffins and rolls every day from Trotter's."

He perked up. "Their almond cinnamon rolls are ex-cellent. I thank you for that, assuming you get in. But no talk of a deal."

"Not even this one?" First I clipped on my ID, then I held out my hand. "Two tickets to tonight's Simone Sanchez concert. She gave them to me herself. As you can imagine, they are excellent seats." I didn't know that, but why would they be anything else? "Please let us in."

Miller took the tickets, checked them out, and nodded ever so slightly. "This," he said, "is a complication. A very attractive complication." His eyebrows arched. "So you did meet her? This also was being discussed in the cafe-teria."

I nodded. "Met her and rode in her car." I reclaimed the tickets. He reluctantly let them slide out of his hand.

Miller inhaled deeply and straightened his shoulders. "Please wait until I've gone in to punch the clock and come back to relieve Petey. He'll head inside to punch out. We all have to punch as we come and go; it's that type of job, I'm sad to say. Sixty years old, I'm still punch-ing the clock. I don't want him to be guilty of anything, so we'll wait 'til he's gone. Then I'll wave you on in if it's clear to do so. If yesterday's memo is still posted, watch for something else. They'd see you on the camera and be here in a flash. They'd freeze the elevator door and have you like that." He snapped his fingers.

"What do we do, then?"

He chewed on a lip, then gave us instructions. "Watch for me to stand on a stool and try to adjust the air vent. Time to time, it closes and gets stuck. We complain, but does it get fixed? It does not. When I stand on the stool, the camera is blocked. You go through then. The tickets?"

I held them back. "I'll leave them on your desk as we pass through."

I did, and as he banged on the vent, he called out his thanks and said, "Looks like they're still hot on your tail." Then he added, "Don't forget the sweet rolls."

"Will he be fired?" Tom asked.

"If he is, Kit will find him something better," I said, hitting the button on the service elevator. Where he doesn't punch a clock, I promised myself.

"She can make that happen?"

"That and more," I said. "Which is why you're here, remember?"

Kit's producer, Tyler, was outside the elevator when we emerged. His jaw dropped and his coffee mug tipped. Whipped cream slid over the edge onto his shirt and he swore. I grabbed Tom by the hand and hurried past. "Hey, Tyler," I said cheerfully. "Seven o'clock, isn't that early for you?" Of course, how would I know, I thought as I rushed toward Kit's office suite. I'm hardly ever here before noon.

"Kelly—" Tyler called. I waved him off as I unlocked and opened the door. I pushed Tom into the outer office, closed and locked the door. Home free.

I pointed to the sofa beside my desk. "Lie down and sleep while you can."

"I want to call my uncle. You said I could."

What did it matter now? I smiled at him. "Your wish is granted. There's the phone. You don't need to dial nine. Tell him—"

Tom's jaw dropped, his eyes widened. I turned.

Kit stood in the doorway of her office. She shrieked, "You did it!" She danced a little jig. "You outfoxed those bastards and you did it." She gathered herself with a deep breath and held out her hand. "Your Highness. I'm Kit Carpenter."

Tom pulled his gaze away from her claw, looked her in the eye, and took the hand. "It's very nice to meet you, Ms. Carpenter. By the way, I'd like to marry your niece," he said. "Or kill her."

Kit threw her head back and laughed. "Can't do either, my lovely boy. I need her." Then she turned to me, wagged the claw, and said, "I love you. Oh, how I love you."

Tom made his call to his uncle, stating his plans. I wasn't sure how the conversation went, because I had herded Kit into her office and closed the door.

She started shooting off orders: "Notes, I need the Lakveria notes from yesterday's show. Where did I put them? Have you filed them already? They should cover it all, but anything else you've learned from the prince I want to know. I want to know all of it, everything he said, everything you got out of him. Tell me about your night. Oh, honey, tell me everything."

"The first thing you should know is that it's cool with Simone. Tyler needs to call her assistant and reschedule."

"We'll get to her later. I want to hear about your night."

"We hung out and went to a movie. Two movies. Kit, quit dancing, would you please quit dancing around and listen?" She stood still and grinned. The Kit who swallowed the canary. So pleased with herself, as if she was the one who'd reeled him in.

"He believes he's all set to do the show, but his people can swoop in here anytime and take him away. I have to believe they'll try. And if they do, he won't argue. He'll go quietly. He's worried, he's obedient, he doesn't want to harm the negotiations. Kit, you can't be rough with him because he'll fold up, he'll shut down on you."

She nodded. "Then draft me some notes. Tell me how to handle him. You obviously have that figured out."

"I've given you all I know about Lakveria. As to how to handle him, I just told you: Go easy." I sighed. "Assuming they let you get that far."

"But right now he says he's willing to talk?"

"Yes."

"Then why let him call? Why not spring a surprise?"

"Because I promised, Kit. Because it would be wrong. How bad was it around here yesterday?"

Kit's laugh rolled out. "The boys were a bit upset, dear. The spineless number–crunching bastards aren't used to dealing with phone calls from the State Department and visits from Lakverian security."

"I figured it didn't take them long to follow a trail back to the station. I called you here and at home around six. When I didn't even get your voice mail, I suspected they were watching closely. They covered the house, too, right?"

She reached out and patted the few tufts of my day–old hair that remained standing. "Did you know that *Vogue* says the bob is back?"

"Kit, please pay attention."

"They watched, dear. I doubt if they went so far as to tap into my phone, but I imagine they had their little listening devices out in the car. Clever of you to anticipate that. I knew you would. They were there all night. I took cookies out to them before I went to bed. It was all very courteous, though; no one wanted an incident." She sat at her desk. "I need to go over some things and you need to write down what you learned from Prince Tomas." She looked up. "He seems very young, Kelly. Far too young to have to deal with being a king. I imagine you know everything about him now. After a whole night together you must have learned it all. I *want* it all. And send him down to Raoul, would you? He keeps clean shirts in his office; make him give one to the boy. He'll interview better if he feels fresher." Kit started thumbing through papers. I recognized my own notes, with their color-coded system of questions and prompts.

I paused at the door, my hand on the knob. "Kit, there will be a price to pay, you have to know that. You can't do what we did and not concede something. There'll be consequences for everyone. Tom, especially. But you and me, too. We'll have to pay, too."

Kit's cheerful demeanor went steely. "So you think we might get slapped for chasing a story? You think it might cost us something? Well, stop the presses!" She wagged her claw again, this time not so affectionately. "Don't you lecture me about the sacrifices in this business, Kelly, don't ever do that."

"I don't mean to lecture you, Kit. It's just a caution. This will cost us."

She smiled again as she looked down at the papers. "Go," she said softly.

Tom was staring at the phone. He looked beaten, like he'd blasted curfew or been caught with a six-pack and a girl in his room.

"Talk to your uncle?" I asked.

He nodded.

"Pretty upset?"

He nodded.

"Are you sure you still want to do this?"

Tom looked at me. "Of course I do. But I agreed that he could come down and . . ." He dropped his head in his hands.

"Monitor the interview?"

Tom looked up. "He can watch and listen. He's not coming alone, Kelly. He's bringing General Kolar and the prime minister. He was furious. What I did last night was so frivolous. Irresponsible. If it gets out—"

"That's just the exhaustion talking. What you did last night was good clean fun. And what you're about to do is the smartest diplomatic move anyone has come up with." He didn't look convinced. "Okay," I said, sighing. "Here's the spin you put on it, because I know Kit, and I know she'll say something about us being out all night. It will get out. So you say to America . . ." I closed my eyes and spun the words. "Tell the radio world that you were out soaking up the American freedom and spirit, and it's your dream—and intention—to make sure Lakverian people will be able to enjoy nothing less."

Oh, what a lovely baritone laugh. "That's a bit thick, Kelly. I can't say that," he said.

I hauled him up by the arm. "You can if you're wearing a nice clean shirt."

Raoul and Tyler were holding up the wall in the hall outside the office. They sprang to attention when we emerged. "Hi, guys," I said. "This is the prince and he needs a clean shirt and I'm sorry for the trouble yesterday but today's show will be great."

Raoul waved it all away. "I don't like being threatened

by thugs, foreign or US. Along about six last night I started cheering you on, Kelly. Grateful, I might add, that I could claim I was totally innocent." He looked Tom over and said, "Sixteen thirty-three?"

"Close enough," replied His Highness.

"By the way, Raoul," I called out as he and Tom walked away, "you'd better tell them downstairs that we're expecting a king." He stopped in his tracks and turned slowly around. I nodded. "And he won't be alone."

Kit had closed the door between our offices, which meant she was cramming. Fine. Best, really, that she didn't know what I was about to do. I flipped through the Rolodex, punched in the numbers, looked at my watch while the phone rang at the other end. Okay, I thought. So she thinks she knows everything about sacrifice. "Good morning," I said when I heard the voice. "This is Kelly Ray, Kit Carpenter's niece? I'm sorry to bother you on a day like this and so early, but, sir, I thought it best, if you haven't already heard, that you know what's happening. And I need some help."

The king and his men arrived twenty minutes before show time. I'd just returned from delivering rolls and coffee to Miller. His booth was a calm oasis, and I was tempted to linger, but it was just delaying the inevitable. When I got back to the eleventh floor, I ran head-on into an army of security people.

King Mikel was an older bald version of Tom. I'd like to say we hit it off, but the once-over he laid on me was pure arctic air. Cold—cold and pissed. Well, why not? I'd spent the night with his nephew. For all he knew, I was at that moment incubating yet another future king. For all he knew—

"Good morning, Kelly." I looked past the royalty to the open office door as the former vice president of the United States walked in. "Vice President Ripley," I said, "thank you for coming. Everyone, thank you for coming. I realize all this is not on the conference schedule. I hope that it doesn't cause a problem." I counted heads. "Shouldn't there be one more?"

King Mikel said, "We decided that the prime minister should attend the breakfast as planned." He glared at his nephew. "The work of the conference is not finished."

"Then you probably all want something to eat. Please, there's coffee and baked goods." My lame hostessing ended when Kit burst upon us. Her initial jubilation upon entering the office and seeing the king and his general was somewhat dampened when she noticed her neighbor standing behind the Lakverian brass. She greeted the Europeans graciously, maybe even humbly, though that might have been acting. Then she turned to the former vice president of the United States.

He said, "Hello, Kit."

She said, "Hello, Allen." Then she glared at me.

Kit outlined her plan: She'd do two segments with Prince Tomas before opening the phones during the third; then, after the long on-the-hour commercial break, she'd do three segments with the elders.

The general was the first to respond. Not surprisingly, it was an order. "This cannot extend beyond eleven; His Highness, the prime minister, and Prince Tomas must be in New York by late afternoon."

She shrugged. "Of course it won't run over; 'Sports Watch' is next."

He nodded. "And we want to sit alongside Prince Tomas. No one will speak until it's our segment, but in case he needs prompting or help with the facts, we should be at his side."

"No," Kit said. "Not negotiable."

Peace was maintained when Tyler suggested that the onlookers watch from his booth while Tom and Kit talked in hers. Everyone seemed pleased enough, so we headed to the studio. Raoul went ahead with a pair of security men.

KLIP has two broadcast studios. One's new, state-of-the art, and located on the ground floor. Wide picture windows open to the sidewalk and street, and speakers let passersby listen as well as watch.

Kit works out of the basement studio, the only KLIP host to still use the old place. As we settled in, I gently tapped the glass separating producer from star. Was it strong enough to hold back the general if he heard something he didn't like? Tyler brought in three extra chairs. On the other side of the glass Kit was helping Prince Tom with his headphones and microphone—all a pantomime to us, because she'd turned off the mike. Just as Tyler signaled the two-minute warning, Raoul's secretary hurried in, carrying rolls and coffee. The king looked pleased, and after studying the pastries at length, he made his decision and settled back into his chair with decaf and a sticky bun.

Three, two, one . . .

Once again Kit blew me away. She had world leaders in the room, the fate of a nation was in their hands, the diplomatic stakes were heaven high, and she, of course, played it her way.

"Welcome to 'Kit Chat,' this is Kit Carpenter. My dear people, if you're still mad at me because Simone Sanchez wasn't on the show yesterday, take heart. We've rescheduled her for another morning. We'll be announcing that date during tomorrow's show. So would you please stop with the calls and e-mails? No more complaints, I'm not in the mood. Want to know why?"

Did it matter?

"You've all heard me talk about my niece, Kelly."

One of the reasons I chose not to listen to "Kit Chat."

"She didn't come home last night. You parents out there, you know the feeling, right? Well, you all know I don't have children, she's all I've got, and yesterday I spent the night wondering where she was and when I'd see her. No, it's not what you're thinking. She's fine, I couldn't be prouder. Yesterday, America, she had a night on the town with a prince. A gorgeous, charming young man who happens to be the future king of Lakveria. A very gorgeous, very charming young man who happens to be sitting with me right now. Crown Prince Tomas Teronovich, welcome to 'Kit Chat.' Talk now."

Tom was so stunned that he could barely say hello. Beside me, General Kolar growled. Kit charged on. "Sure, you're of Lakverian heritage, sure, you're the male descendent of a long line of kings, but dear boy, you were born in Paris, raised in Texas—that explains the accent you'll hear, America, if he ever opens his mouth—and you've been going to college in Great Britain. Why in the world should you be king of a very troubled Eastern European country?"

That was no better. Tom, haltingly, spoke of the election, the Lakverian people's expressed desire for a unifying force while rebuilding democracy.

Kit said, "Uh-huh. Think it will work?"

Oh, he tried. Answer by answer, he tried. But under her eye, knowing even as he stumbled that she had another question waiting, he spoke with the enthusiasm of someone walking through a bed of scorpions.

It was mighty chilly in our booth.

I edged forward to Tyler. "Give me Kit's headphone, just hers." He tapped a switch and I was in her head. I said into the mike, "Ask him about his sister, Natalia. Ask him about the work she was doing."

King Mikel and the general made noises.

Kit waited while Tom finished giving a stock overview of the UN peacekeeping mission. Then she said, "Tell me about your sister."

Radio rule number one: Silence is the enemy. Tom was very silent. Kit filled the dead air with a prompt: "What work was she doing?" Tom turned in his seat and looked directly at me. The radio waves emanating from KLIP might have been empty at that moment, but his look was loaded. He turned back and faced Kit, took a breath and said, "Yes, we should talk about my sister."

From then, it was golden.

I fed her a couple more questions, but they were hardly needed, and by the time Tom was discussing the work in the refugee camps that his sister had been doing, they'd found their groove. And by the time Tyler cued the first commercial break, Tom and my aunt were talking with the earnest energy of reconciling lovers.

The vice president poured another round of coffee; the king helped himself to a muffin.

Round two went even better. By then the phone lines were lit all across the board, and Tyler and his assistant were screening the calls, lining them up like planes ready for takeoff.

With just a few minutes to go before the end of the segment, Tyler turned to me and tapped his headset. "This one wants you, Kelly," he said.

I shook my head. "You know my rule, Tyler: Kit can talk *about* me, but no one ever talks *to* me."

"Caller says she owes you something. She asked for the delivery girl."

I stepped to the board, put on an extra headset, and said, "Good morning, Simone."

"He sounds just like a king should sound, don't you think?"

"Yes, he does."

"Of course, he's not a king yet, but you've got him that much closer. Maybe, just maybe, things might not fall apart completely before he gets his chance. So, congratulations, Delivery Girl."

"You give me too much credit. Without you, it wouldn't have happened. Don't you want to speak with him?"

"Not a good idea, I think. They're on to something pretty serious—can't you hear? Refugees and health clinics. If I butt in, it will all get off track."

"That's true."

"Besides, it was you I wanted to speak with. Was it a wonderful night? Tell me it was, Delivery Girl, it's the only answer I want."

"All right then: It was a wonderful night." Behind me, the king and his men shifted. Someone cleared his throat. "And how was the house, Simone? Was that wonderful, too?"

She sighed. "I stayed for two hours. I had supper there, right in her kitchen. Yes, it was wonderful. I took loads of pictures; they're being developed now. Come backstage tonight after the show and I'll show them to you."

Oops. No tickets. "I might need to sleep."

"Nonsense. And I want to give you a copy of the photo of the three of us; I always get doubles."

"Simone, I gave away the tickets to someone who helped me and Tom. But I'd love the photo."

"Then you'll have to come get it. I'll send over more tickets. You sound blue and down, Delivery Girl. But why? You got what you wanted."

"Yes, I did," I said softly.

"Of course," she replied, "those are the things that are painful to lose. And now your wonderful night is over."

"I suppose it is."

"Then all you can do is make this next one even better, so come to my show. Good-bye, Kelly Ray. Give my love to Prince Tom."

I handed the headset to Tyler and stepped back to my place by the wall. In the booth Kit was wildly gesturing, the claw catching the light and flashing. I smiled. Maybe Kit would go to the concert with me, go backstage and meet her diva double. I caught my breath as I pictured the scene. Those two in the same room? Maybe not.

Raoul entered the booth and whispered in my ear. "Is that a good idea?" I replied aloud.

Vice President Ripley said, "Is what a good idea?"

"A reporter and cameraman from our affiliate television station would like to step in and observe and later talk with any of you gentlemen," Raoul said. He turned to me. "And you, too, Kelly. They're interested in you."

"I'm not the story, Raoul. Not a chance."

The politicians consulted while I tried to listen to Kit and Tom. I heard the Veep say, "He's doing very well." A few murmured words more, then Vice President Ripley nodded to Raoul, who quickly left the booth. He returned within seconds with two men, a glossy groomed reporter and a bearded giant with a camera perched on his shoulder. Everyone but the king shifted to make room.

"Isn't there a Marx Brothers movie that goes like this?" I said aloud.

"*A Night at the Opera*," said my neighbor the statesman.

"No, I think she means *Monkey Business*," the camera guy said. His camera whirred and he pointed it at me. I clasped my hands on my head and hid behind my elbows.

Kit noticed the new activity. Any publicity is good publicity; she smiled broadly and made a clapping motion. Tom turned and looked; his face was pained. The camera whirred away.

I peeked over Tyler's shoulder and looked at the phone log. "Are the callers friendly?"

He nodded. "Some in tears; among the eight on hold, we've got three Lakverian refugees living in Dakota City."

I fed Kit another prompt: "Tell them they can make a difference. Tell them to call their representatives and demand the UN pledge be paid."

Which is the plea Tom made just before Tyler cued them for the long mid-show break. The On Air light went out and the men in the booth with me applauded. Kit rose, stretched, did her little jig. Tom slumped.

Tyler began prepping the king and the general for their part of the show. I excused myself and went into the other booth.

"It's going well," I said. Kit didn't need to be told that, of course. Tom looked as if he didn't believe it, or as if he'd been awake all night. "Do I look as bad as you?" I asked.

"Worse," he said. "I have a clean shirt."

Tyler poked his head in. "We need to get set up. Can I bring in chairs?"

I held up my hand. "Just a minute." He shrugged and closed the door. Beyond the glass the men were smoothing ties and patting pockets. Primping, as if Kit's audience would be able to see them.

I faced my aunt, eye to eye. "Don't bring them on."

"What?"

"Don't bring in the old men. You cannot turn this over to them. It will ruin what you've got going. Just keep it this way, you and Tom and your listeners. Please, Kit. Don't bring in the old men."

I turned to Prince Tom. He was shaking his head slightly. "Kelly, I promised."

"You can do what you want, Tom. You make the decision. But this is the best way, I know it is. You and Kit, no one else."

Kit swore, drummed her fingers on the artificial arm, and then said, "She's right. She's absolutely right, Your Highness. It's good politics for you and even better radio for me. Look at those old coots: You can just feel the hot air getting ready to blow. Yes, it's exactly what we should do, but, my dear boy, are you up to it? Another fifty minutes?"

He thought, nodded, and then a little boy's smile spread across his face. "But would someone else tell my uncle?"

Kit and I pointed at each other as we both said, "You."

She flicked her mike switch. "Tyler, tell the gentlemen that they can sit back down. Thank you." She switched off.

"That's it?" I said.

"The rest is up to you, dear," she said. "If you think it's such a good idea that I dump these world leaders, you can explain it to them. You go make it right, Kelly. I may want them back here someday, so you make it right." She flopped into her seat. "Oh, yeah. This one will cost me."

I bit back a smile. Wait 'til she knew exactly how much.

"By the way, hon, what's with Brant Butler showing up with his cameraman?"

"Raoul's idea." I tapped Tom's arm gently. "Simone called. She's listening; she sends her love. We both think you're doing great." Then I escaped.

Tyler cued the start just as I slipped back into the production booth. "What's up, Kelly?" he said.

I took a deep breath and smiled at the men before turning to Raoul. "Could you get them out of here?" I motioned toward the TV guys. "Please? Maybe they could set up the interview space somewhere?"

As soon as they were gone, I faced the vice president. "The prince and Kit think it's better to keep going with just the two of them."

He raised his eyebrows. "She's bouncing us?" I nodded. "You call me this morning to ask—to plead—that I skip an important breakfast and come on your aunt's show with His Highness and General Kolar. You start my day by telling me that you've got the missing prince all set to go on national radio and would I mind coming down to smooth troubled waters."

"Yes, and thank you very much."

"And now you want to bounce us all."

"Her listeners are probably burning up the phone lines to DC now, sir. Do you want to risk shutting that down?"

Vice President Ripley had been talking with a stern diplomat's posture; still, there was a hint of a smile, and it blossomed now. "Do you really think I mind not going on the air with her?" He turned to the others. "Your Highness. General. She's right. Kit Carpenter's listeners are legion and they take action. Best, really, we let this continue as it is."

The king of Lakveria was watching the interview. He nodded. "Tomas is doing fine; as you say."

The general didn't speak. He might not have agreed, but his vote didn't count.

Tyler shot me a look, then stared down at the board.

"Caller on two, Kit," he said. "She arrived in the States three weeks ago from Lakveria. Name is Ana, says she lost all three of her children, killed by rebel guerrillas."

Kit opened the call, welcoming the woman, gently leading her into the conversation.

"Switch me to the prince," I asked Tyler. I leaned into the mike. "Hey, Tommy, it's me. Don't talk, your mike is on." He turned and looked. "Everything's fine, they're all very pleased." Tom looked toward his great-uncle. The king dipped his head.

"By the way, Kelly," the vice president whispered when I stepped back in my place, "Mrs. Ripley and I are delighted about the tree. Surprised, but delighted."

"I'm glad you're both happy. As soon as I got off the phone with you, I called the service you recommended and left a message. It should be down today."

"Your aunt does know, doesn't she, Kelly?"

"It will be fine, Mr. Vice President. I promise."

My neighbor laughed. "Suddenly I'm very optimistic about world peace. It seems small enough, compared to other problems I've tackled."

"How can you be?" I said sharply. He sobered abruptly. "I'm sorry, sir, but are you listening to these callers? Are all of you listening to their stories? The horrible things that have happened—there's no hope the enemies will reconcile. How can one side ever forget what the other did? And him." I pointed to Tom. "He's going to be destroyed, isn't he? One way or another, whether he's crushed or he's killed, he won't survive. What are the chances he'll survive? He doesn't believe he will."

King Mikel turned around and stared at me.

"I can't say, Kelly," replied my neighbor. "I'll be frank about that. The rebel faction will be after him and it may succeed. Some day, some sniper or guerrilla bomb might find its target. Yes, they will go after him as they went after his sister. Hope is their enemy, and that's what Tomas and Natalia represent. But, as you say, he knows that. He knows—we all know—that it's a dangerous business, building peace and making it last."

"But you keep trying. It doesn't ever seem to be working anywhere, but you keep trying, you all keep banging your heads against a very hard wall."

"There's no other option."

I looked at him. "How can you keep going?"

His blue eyes locked onto mine and held me by their kind sadness and concern. "Day by day, Kelly. It's all just day by day."

The scene after the show was a zoo. Raoul tried to herd everyone to his office, but the general had other ideas. "The airport . . ." he kept saying. Brant Butler and his cameraman emerged from a room, the camera still whirring. They were followed by six bodyguards. I spotted the thugs who had frisked me at the hotel and waved. When Kit and Tom joined us, there was applause all around. Kit blew me a kiss and mouthed "Thank you" before turning toward the camera. Over the din, the general could be heard. "The airport, please, the airport . . ."

I checked my watch. Five past eleven. I, too, should've been somewhere else.

"Kelly." I looked up and saw Tom pushing his way through the crowd.

"Your Highness," said the general, "we must leave now."

"Prince Tomas," said the king, "you must have a word with the press."

He ignored them. We stood eye to eye as they all crowded around.

"I have to be going," he said.

"Yes, you do," I replied. "The UN awaits. Can you sleep on a plane? I sure hope so."

He shook his head impatiently and leaned toward me. "I wish . . ." He inhaled and exhaled, one long noisy sigh. He opened and closed his mouth twice, not finding what it was he wanted to say.

"I think we're both all talked out, Prince Tomas," I said. "Your people are waiting, so let's just say good—"

He held up a hand and shushed me. "I wish," he whispered, "I wish that I'd kissed you last night."

I glanced at the camera that was aimed at us, then I looked back at those eyes and said softly, "I wish you had, too."

And then, with as strong a rush as I've ever felt, a thousand other wishes crowded my head: Be safe, be happy, may your sister heal, be safe, I hope you get your hands on Charlemagne's map, I hope there will be peace in Lakveria, be safe, be safe, be safe.

He started to speak, but couldn't, so instead, he made a princely move. He took my hand in his and raised it to his lips.

The camera caught it all; there were witnesses galore. I'm certain, though, that no one but me saw his eyes change color, no one else knew how tightly he squeezed, and no one could see my thumb stroking his hand as he lowered mine from the kiss.

He stared at the back of my hand. "Look at me, Tommy," I whispered. He raised his eyes.

I said, "Be good at what you do." And then I stepped back and let go.

The eleven o'clock meeting was well under way when I reached St. Ambrose's. My usual spot near the back was empty, but after scanning the room, I walked right past that chair and slid into an empty one next to Sandi. She narrowed her eyes and watched me settle. I caught her glance, then at the same time we both whispered, "You okay?"

"I'm good," she said. "But you look terrible."

"Running on fumes."

The speaker was deep into her story by then, so we clammed up. It was the usual thing—different in the details, but identical in outline: a life ripped apart by drugs, a life rebuilt one day at a time. I closed my eyes while I listened. Listened.

When the speaker was done, we shifted into a round robin, starting at the front. Sandi leaped right up. She was more family than friend to most of the people there, and was greeted warmly. She talked about her night. I'd seen her, of course, so I had a picture to go with the description of her close call, of the evening spent hanging by a thread.

"This time yesterday, well, most of you saw me then, I was happy as could be, top of the world. Such as it is, my world. After the meeting some of us went to lunch, and, oh, we were so loud at the restaurant, laughing and telling stories, that all the other diners couldn't wait to see us go. When I did go, I headed home to call my girl, Tami. It was her birthday . . ." She paused, her hand bobbing in the space in front of her, as if abandoned midair when she lost her thought. She pulled it all in. "Everyone here knows what I mean when I say that it sure doesn't take long to get off track. Plenty of us here have crashed. Just one night goes bad and we crash, lose all we've built up. You can do all the work, you can run the program, but still you crash. And it can happen so fast. I came that close last night. One of those nights, right? Who hasn't had one? Well, it was last night for me. I came that close, that close. But a talk with a friend, a phone call, and I held on. And now I've got another day, one more day clean and sober."

I'd always thought that if I ever got up to speak and offered more than what Sandi called name tag stuff, it would be a rush—a mind-blowing, sweaty-palm, nerve-wracking rush. And it probably would have been, if I weren't so tired.

There's a drill to the round robin. You identify yourself and then say as much or as little as you have in you. Plenty of people never get too far past their name. I never really had before and today I almost didn't again. I was about to drop back down in my seat when I heard the familiar voice, heard Kit, heard her command echo in my head: *Talk now!*

"I just want to add to what Sandi said," I started. "It's so true, how it can all fall apart so fast. You crash before you even knew you were headed somewhere." People nodded, and I heard a few murmurs of agreement. "But it can go the other way, just as quickly. You can get through something—a night, or a day, or a phone call, maybe, and suddenly you see how far you've come. And I think that's good to talk about, too."

I dropped back down into my seat. In a moment Sandi pulled me over to rest on her shoulder. In another moment I was fast asleep.

The noise of people folding up the metal chairs woke me. When I shook the sleep from my head, I saw that Sandi was gone and I was laid out on three chairs with someone's shoulder bag for a pillow. I sat up and looked around. Sandi was standing with a group near the door. She saw me and came over.

"I'm not inviting you to join us for lunch today because you need to go home and take care of yourself. Go get some real sleep." She turned to a man collecting chairs in the row behind me. "Did you listen to 'Kit Chat'?" She tipped her head toward me. "She was up all night with a prince."

The guy wasn't interested. He just pointed and said, "I need those chairs now."

Sandi said, "I'll see you tomorrow, Kelly. Take care of yourself, that's number one. Do you hear me: Take care."

"Yes," I said, "that's what I'll do."

The houses around Lake Lucille are even grander in daylight. Mostly because of the gardens. Like the houses, the Lake Lucille gardens are larger and more elaborate than any others in the city. And this late in June, the flower beds were really exploding.

The house at Twenty-seventh and Lake Drive was awash in color. I'm not much into flowers, but I knew a few, and I knew that the white and red things were peonies and I knew that they were spectacular. The delphinium was going nuts, too. Not surprising: It was always her favorite.

I tapped a blossom and it bobbed. A droopy bush with round white flowers was overhanging the steps. I brushed against it as I climbed.

Seven steps, then the long walk to the house, more steps, cross the porch, knock. That's all you have to do. Don't stop now, Kelly, not here, keep going. She might slam—

"What are you doing here?"

I stopped on the top step. Caught my breath, then turned.

She was kneeling amid some flowers. She rose, brushed dirt off her jeans, and walked toward me, clutching a sharp-pointed trowel in her hand.

She's a tall woman. We're the same height, have been since I was thirteen. People used to say the typical dumb things about how much alike we looked, sisters almost. She loved it, once.

"I said, what are you doing here?"

So there we were: face to face for the first time in two years. Her holding a potential weapon and me sleep-deprived, unwashed, and mute. Advantage: hers.

She tried a different tack. "I listened to Kit today. Sounds like you had quite a night."

That roused me. Couldn't cough up any words, but something must have shown on my face. She arched an eyebrow, shrugged, and said, "I tune in occasionally. Sometimes she . . . is interesting."

And sometimes she . . . talks about me. I licked my lips. "Your irises look good. The garden is already much nicer than when Grandma lived here."

"Cut it out, Kelly. Get to the point." She closed the space between us (still holding the trowel) until we were standing eye to eye. I breathed in . . .

And laughed. That scent, oh my gosh, there it was, now I knew. Confixor, her favorite styling lotion, I recog-

nized it now. *Styling lotion.* Oh, Tommy, I thought. You little Gypsy prince; you use Aveda hair products.

She wasn't laughing at my private joke, of course. She
said, "Kelly, I don't see what's so funny. You show up at
my home unannounced and there is nothing funny."

I composed myself, sobered, and stood tall. Now she
slumped and softened and looked about while she
seemed to search for words. "You have this wild night,
you show up here when two years ago we all agreed you
wouldn't ever do so, and you . . . you look like you've
been through hell." She drew herself up, but I could tell
it took all her effort. "Why are you here?" she whispered.

Did I know? "Please . . ." I could see that she wouldn't
help, this would be up to me. Try again. "Please, I . . ." And
again. "I want . . ."

What's the hardest thing you've ever done?
Confess to something stupid? Something bad?
Walk into a classroom, the new kid in school?
Say no to drugs?
Say "Get lost" to a boyfriend, say good-bye to a friend?
End an abusive thing you once called love?
If you've done any of that, then good for you,
Because all of it's hard, and some of it's very hard.
And what was the hardest thing for Kelly Ray?
Well, it might not look that tough, but believe me, it was.
She admitted to something.
She admitted to wanting. She acknowledged desire,

Deep-buried desire.
And with no reason at all—not one in the world—
To think she'd be allowed what she wanted,
She stood there and said
    Please . . .
Hard as it was, she said
    Please, I . . .
She dug down and said
    I want . . .
Say it, Kelly Ray. Take a deep breath and say it.
    "Please, I want . . .
    "Please, Mom. I want to see my sister."